THE HAUNTING PACT

JULIANNE RIVERS

Copyright © 2024 by [Author or Pen Name]

All rights reserved.

No portion of this book may be reproduced in any form without written permission from the publisher or author, except as permitted by U.S. copyright law.

Contents

1. Chapter 1   1
2. Chapter 2   5
3. Chapter 3   10
4. Chapter 4   15
5. Chapter 5   21
6. Chapter 6   31
7. Chapter 7   35
8. Chapter 8   40
9. Chapter 9   45
10. Chapter 10   51
11. Chapter 11   54
12. Chapter 12   59
13. Chapter 13   62
14. Chapter 14   72

15.	Chapter 15	77
16.	Chapter 16	82
17.	Chapter 17	86
18.	Chapter 18	92
19.	Chapter 19	98
20.	Chapter 20	108
21.	Chapter 21	113
22.	Chapter 22	118
23.	Chapter 23	124
24.	Epilogue	136

Chapter 1

"Papaaaaa plz Save me! He will take me with him. He causes me a lot of pain!" a girl wearing a white frock with red stains on it and bruises on her face screamed to her parents from her room she was tied to her bed.

"Did you talk to them, when are they coming?" asked the girl's father.

"Papa don't worry. They are coming this time our Munni will be fine" replied the girl's brother.

All the family members were watching the girl scream in the pain. Her mother was crying seeing her daughter in a state like this. Their daughter was possessed by an evil spirit for the last 4 months. And finally, after a lot of psychological help they were calling paranormal help because their daughter was doing unimaginable things which made them into believing that their daughter is actually possessed not mentally ill or abnormal.

Suddenly the main gate of their house opened and a black Vitara breeeza entered. 6 people stepped out of car. A guard saw them and came near them and asked:

Guard: sir you are from paranormal team, right?

Maanvir: "Yes, we were called here. Mr. Singhania's daughter is possessed."

Saina: {with a deep voice} guys her life is in danger can sense it. We need to hurry.

Adhiraj: ok fine it means it's real! Kaka, please take us to the girl. EVERYONE COME NEAR! Executing Mission, no 98 Okay, so Himanshu and I will handle the girl. Saina, try to communicate with her spirit. Alishka, you attempt to gather information from her parents. Ahaan and Maanvir, remove or start all the electrical equipment one by one, and then we three will go inside!

EVERYONE: YES SIR!

Saina, Adhiraj, Himanshu went in while other three stayed out getting ready with equipment's.

Alishka: Singhania's Mansion hmm very rich people in fact I saw Arnav Singhania in a recent party too.

Ahaan: And how that does that help?

Alishka: {frowning} Aree, I saw him four months ago and after that there was an accident of a young man on a road highway, The person who caused the accident was not caught, but as far as I know, their daughter fell ill afterward.

Ahaan: {rolling his eyes} Miss Alisha, you are perhaps a paranormal investigator, not a crime investigator.?

Maanvir: No, Alishka has a point! Alishka, why don't you go and talk to the family members? Maybe we can find some help?

Alishka: ok boss. Aur yes Mr. Jaiswal this info is really important!

Alishka went in. On the other hand, as the three were approaching girls' room, Saina started sensing negativity.

Saina: {with a deep voice} Guys, this spirit is very powerful! I can sense its energies from here. I think Adi we need Alisha's help too.

Adhiraj: Listen Saina try your best because you know that although Aliksha is a sensitive like you but still she is good in chanting prayer and understanding psychology.

Guard: Sir, these people have come. You guys go inside.

As the three entered the room. Seeing the rooms condition they immediate got a current of negativity. Seeing them arrive Mrs. Singhania {girl's mother] came near them and with a sobbing voice she pleaded them to save their daughter.

Himanshu: Aunty, we promise you that we will save your daughter, but for that, you all will also need to perform a certain process!

Listening to this girl's brother came and questioned.

Aranav: hi I am Arnav I only called you guys. You are from Shadow hunters, right?

Saina: {with a hushed voice} we don't have time it's getting stronger and stronger!

Adhiraj: Arnav bhai, we'll meet later. First, you take us to the victim.!

Arnav: ji

Saina: {loudly] ADHIRAJ GET AWAY FROM THERE

As she said those words the girl who was tied to bed suddenly rose up and blood started coming outta her mouth. She started laughing loudly and a devil voice came from her mouth!

Girl: {devil speaking} So, these people have come to save you? Until my revenge is complete, you won't survive. HAHAHAH.

Alishka: {with raised eyebrow} Revenge what kind of revenge? What do you want? Why are you after this innocent person?

Chapter 2

Maanvir: Everyone needs to empty the room, and some work needs to be done.

Ahaan: {intervenes} First, everyone covers all the mirrors with black-colored clothes. Then, everyone should go as far away from this room as possible. There will also be a shouting sound from inside the room, and no one should enter....

Arnav: Sir? Can I stay please?

Ahaan: {coldly} If you want to stay here, there's only one condition: no matter what happens, do not go near the girl, even by mistake.

Saina: {shouting} AAAA! GUYS, WE HAVE VERY LITTLE TIME. PLEASE HURRY—I WON'T BE ABLE TO HOLD ON MUCH LONGER!

Alishka: {with a slow yet firm voice} Please go outside, everyone. And follow all the instructions.

Every family member left and closed the door behind. Saina signaled Adhiraj and Himanshu to tackle the girl. Adhiraj went near her and caught her by her waist, Himanshu by her hands as she felt the touch she started fidgeting and shouting. Saina came near her and held her by her head as she felt Saina's touch, she tried to kick her through her legs but couldn't.

Saina: {firmly}WHO ARE YOU, WHAT DO YOU WANT.

The girl just fidgeted more and growled at her. She tried her best to get off the two but couldn't. Saina once again asked just the difference this time was that she held her head more tightly and pressed it more.

Saina: MAINE PUCHA KAUN HO TUM? KYUN IS MASOOM KE PICHE PADE HOO!

The girl growled more and started screaming. She started kicking her legs and hands. And this time she kicked Saina right into her stomach making her fall down to floor. She also managed to punch Himanshu in his hips which made him to fall. Seeing all this adhiraj lessened his grip which gave chance to the devil and with full force she pushed adhiraj to the ground.

Maanvir: SANNU! You, ok?

Suddenly the light went out and whole room was dark. Adhiraj tried to search for the girl in the bed and near it the girls was nowhere to be find. Alishka started feeling a little pull in her hairs, she immediately turned around to find that the girl was in the air and she was holding her hair in her hand. The girl's eyes were all red, there was a wicked smile in her lips.

Ahaan: {shouting} ALISHAA BE CAREFUL!

Alishka: {shouting} What do you want? Why are you lying behind it?

Girl {devil speaking} "How will you save her when you yourself are prey to some past?!

Alishka: I can help you! I can bring justice to you! Leave this innocent one.

Devil: No! His brother took my life away. I will take his!

Alishka: Anand? Is it you? I heard that you were quite compassionate. Leave her; I promise your revenge will be fulfilled if you just let her go!

Devil: {shaking} HOW……DO YOU…KNOW?

Adhiraj: {whispering}

Ahaan: haan!

Devil: WHAT CAN YOU DO? MY WHOLE FAMILY WAS WAITING FOR ME THAT DAY. HOW WILL YOU BRING BACK THE HAPPINESS OF MY 9-YEAR-OLD DAUGHTER, WHO WAS SO HAPPY TO SEE HER FATHER AFTER SO MANY DAYS?

Arnav who was standing silently and observing everything finally spoke

Arnav: {raising his hands} Look, Anand, whatever happened that day was wrong, and we regret it now. We can find your parents and your daughter for you! In exchange, please let go of our Munni! I promise!

Alishka: Anand, they realize their mistake! Please, kindly let Munni go!

Devil: FINE! I WILL LET HER GO, BUT ONLY FOR 1 HOUR. IF YOUR PROMISE ISN'T FULFILLED BY THEN, I WILL KILL HER, AND AT THAT MOMENT, I WILL END YOUR FAMILY TOO!

Saying this girl left Alisha's hairs and was going to fall to the ground but in the nick of time Alishka caught her. And all the lights came. Maanvir saw Saina lying unconscious in the ground. He ran towards her. Adhiraj saw Himanshu trying to get up but couldn't get up due to pain in his hips he went to help him. Ahaan came towards Alishka as she handed over the girl to Arnav

Himanshu: Brother, she has beaten me badly. I don't think I'll be able to walk.

Adhiraj: {jokingly} How did it feel to get kicked by a 15-year-old girl?

Ahaan: {sternly} Arnav, don't forget that we don't have much time left.!

Arnav: haan! Mamma, Papa! Plz come in.

Mrs. Singhania: {taking the girl from his hand} "is my Munni been alright? Please tell me."

Girl: {feeble voice} Mumma he is gone!

Mrs. Singhania: {sobbing} "Thank you very much to all of you for saving the happiness of this house!"

Ahaan: {coldly} It's not over till yet! Arnav!

Mr. Singhania: Wait what?

Arnav: Dad, please forgive me, but I hit Anand on the road four months ago because I was drinking and driving that day, and I hit him with my car...

He explained everything to his father.

Mr. Singhania: {devastated} Aren't you ashamed? It's a disgrace to call you, my son! If you had helped him, we wouldn't have to see this day!

Ahaan: Sir, we don't have time, please! Otherwise, all our hard work will go to waste.

Mrs. Singhania: "Yes, they are right. Bring his parents and his daughter, otherwise, we'll lose Munni again!"

Singhania summoned his drivers and reached out to Anand's parents and daughter in their village. They received exceptional care and attention. Anand's daughter found a new home with the Singhania family, while his parents were embraced as if they were Mrs. Singhania's own kin. Witnessing this compassionate act, Anand's soul finally found peace and gently departed. Each family member rejoiced.

Each member was happy to see this, and all got a good payment from Mr. Singhania.

CHAPTER 3

Sunday 10 am

Alishka: {yawning} Good morning, guys! What's with all the noise? Who plays games this early in the morning!

Adhiraj: {jokingly} Aww, sorry, did we wake up Sleeping Beauty?

Himanshu: {adding} Oh, did you just call her Sleeping Beauty? That title belongs exclusively to Ahaan bhai to call her!

Saying this they both High-fives and laughed!

Alishka: {frowning} You guys will never change, will you?!

Saina: {controlling her laugh} Come on, guys! You too, Alishu, let's have breakfast!

Maanvir: {teasing} Sannu, do you remember when we tried to be just friends for a few months?

Saina: yes! what an adventure!

Adhiraj: {adding} I wonder how they're managing this?

Alishka: {getting irritated} Don't you guys have anything else to do?

Himanshu: {mischievously} When will the day come when we can finally call you "Bhabhi," Alisha?

Alishka: {irritated} Whatever!

To make thing worse Adhiraj and Himanshu started doing acting of two lovers. Alishka palmed her head and watched it all with a little blush. Ahaan who just woke up due to laughter came out and watched it all with same blush and a little anger. None saw him there.

Adhiraj: {as Ahaan} Alishu I love you will you be mine?

Himanshu: {as Alishka} YES! YES! I LOVE YOU TOO AHAAN!

Seeing this they both blushed but didn't say anything. Suddenly Maanvir's eyes caught Ahaan coming he became silent and elbowed Saina too. Seeing change of expression Aliksha followed their eyes to find Ahaan walking towards there was a little smirk in her face. Adhiraj and Himanshu were not facing towards him so they had no idea but seeing the change of expression they became a little terrified and as they felt touch in their Sholder a shiver of fear ran through their spine and they gulped and turned around to find Ahaan glaring at them.

Himanshu: {fearful} Ahaan bhai, don't you wake up at noon?

Adhiraj: {afraid}brother...it...was..his..plan

Ahaan caught them by collar and glared them angrily. Both were shivering and regretting they looked at each other.

Ahaan: {coldly} How many times do I have to explain to you both?

Maanvir: {with lot of efforts} Ahaan....its..ok..yarr

Ahaan glared at him too he stopped speaking and turned away. Alishka started giggling. Adhiraj signaled Himanshu and both of them laid down into Ahaan's feet and spoke "Bhai plz sorry!"

Ahaan: {with a smirk} so Alishu should we forgive them?

Alishka: {laughing} Sure, sure, after all, they're just kids!

With that both of them started laughing. Hearing laughs Adhiraj and Himanshu looked at each other and were confused. Ahaan helped them to get up and went to the dining table. After that there was a dead silence during breakfast.

Ahaan: Alishu by the way we had to go somewhere?

Alishka: {palming her face} Oh yes, in all this nonsense, I completely forgot I have to go to the hospital today to see Mom!

Saina: how's aunty doing?

Alishka: hmm she's fine. I will update ya all later. Ahaan lets go we are getting late!

Ahaan: ok give 5 minutes I will be ready and take out the car

Alishka rose thumbs up and both of them left.

Saina: {a little jealous} I am her friend since class 8 but still she goes everywhere with Ahaan

Maanvir: Oh, I'm here for you! Let's go out somewhere after that!

Adhiraj: {scratching his head} Guys, one thing that I've never quite understood is why Alishka isn't scared of Ahaan at all. I mean, the rest of us are pretty intimidated, but she seems unfazed.

Himanshu: {interrupting}in fact Ahaan is sometimes scared of Alishka, right?

Saina: {with a deep sigh} That's just the way their chemistry is!

Maanvir: It's okay, buddy. Anyway, they're enough for each other. Thanks to Alishka, Ahaan learned to smile a little, remember how much people used to tease our group during our schooling years? Now, thanks to Ahaan, they don't even dare to look at us!

Saina: True that.

Himanshu: And you know what, guys? Our group is really unique and awesome, and I'm proud of each and every one of us.

Adhiraj: By the way am glad that there are no appointments today.

Maanvir: Yes finally got some time to spend with my love.

Himanshu: Dude why cant we see Ahaan and Alishka like this?

Adhiraj: {smirking} I think today you want to eat Ahaan's most known punch.

Everyone just chuckled at this statement. After a short convo everyone started enjoying the Sunday, unaware that this convo was overheard by Alishka. She had tears in her eyes as the news she was going to give in evening, might hurt the group. But it was the only option she was left with.

Chapter 4

Ahaan was Driving the car and Alishka was there scrolling her phone, she was looking at all the group pictures and recalling the memories they had made. She was weakly smiling and trying to control her tears. Ahaan just casually turned towards her and found her tears strolling down her cheeks. Alishka was unaware of this.

Ahaan: {worriedly} what happened Alishu? is everything ok?

Alishka: {narrowing her brows} Yes? Why what happened?

Ahaan: why are you crying?

Alishka: "When was I... {she looks in the mirror} Oh sorry, never mind. Please drive quickly, I need to meet Mom!"

Ahaan: {in his mind} She must be worried, thinking only about her mom!

Ahaan: {comforting her} It's okay, Alishu, I understand. Auntie will recover soon. We'll celebrate her birthday at your place this time, so don't worry at all, okay?

Alishka looked at him with a weak smile, and nodded

Alishka: You know what Ahaan?

Ahaan: {raising his brow} What?

Alishka: main janti hoon upar se kadak, andar se teddy bear ho tum! {know you're tough on the outside, but inside, you're a real softie!}

Ahaan: {cute smile} Haan Haan pata hai but sirf tumahre liye, aur kisi ko batana mat! { yeah, I know, but just for you. Don't tell anyone else.}

They had a good laugh at this statement and finally reached the hospital, Aliksha went into mother room and hugged her tightly while Ahaan was standing outside and talking to her father. Alishka's family shared a good bond with Ahaan. Alisha's Mother was suffering from lung cancer and heavy amount of money was going on her treatment. She was meeting a mom after a long time and seeing her condition worse made her cry. Her mom was happy to see her child after a long time she hugged her and gave her forehead kiss, wiped her tears and assured her that she will be fine. After some time Aliksha came out and her father went in, Ahaan so tears strap on her face and consoled her. They left the hospital after that.

Alishka: Ahaan, I wanted to talk about something serious plz can we stop at a café?

Ahaan: Hmm ok!

After a few minutes of driving they stopped at a cafe, seated themselves and ordered their meal as it was almost lunch. There was an awkward silence between them, Aliksha was lost in her deep thoughts and her fingers were fidgeting between each other seeing this Ahaan finally spoke.

Ahaan: Alishu? Alishkaaaaaa?? Hello???

Alishka: {jolting}, yes?

Ahaan: I think you wanted to talk about something. What happened, is everything okay? Why are you so worried?

Alishka: Dude, Ahaan, um... the thing is... I can't do this anymore. I mean, it's not that I don't want to, but... I just can't!

Ahaan: What do you mean? What can't you do? Stop beating around the bush and just tell me clearly what's going on.

Alishka: {taking a deep breath} Ahaan I can't do Paranormal investigating anymore!

Ahaan: {shocked} but why? I thought you loved your job.

Alishka: Ahaan, I do love my job! But the thing is, it's about the future, my career, and most importantly, financial issues! You see, Dad has invested all his insurance and savings in Mom's treatment. Now, there's nothing left. And earlier, Aleena... {her voice chokes} she used to manage things as she was a manager at a company with a good salary, but she's not here anymore, and I don't have any siblings who can help with expenses! Moreover, as a paranormal investigator, our earnings are limited. Yes, enough to cover our own expenses, but what about our parents? I know... I started all this... but {starts sobbing} I'm sorry, I can't do it anymore!

Seeing her cry Ahaan changed his seat and sat behind her, held her hand and gave his Sholder to cry.

Alishka: {still sobbing} I never wanted to leave... in fact, it was my dream that we... always stay together... and our certificates have the same career written on them... but circumstances are such...

Ahaan: Alishu I understand! But there must be another way, right?

Alishka: {sour voice} Ahaan I did try my best to find another way but there is no way!

Ahaan: Okay, tell me one thing, if you quit this, then what will you do?

Listening to this Aliksha took out her phone and showed him a job appointment letter.

Ahaan: {shocked} You've been offered a job as a manager at INDIA BASKET {fictional} and that too from Delhi? But when did you apply for it?

Alishka: I didn't my father did! And that too without my permission.

Ahaan: Alishka you really want to leave. I mean we can find a way yarr.

Alishka: I am sorry Ahaan!

Ahaan was really shocked to hear this news they had their lunch and didn't speak. While driving the car they were again a dead silence in the car Ahaan was lost in his whole world. While Alishka was preparing herself to how to give a good explanation to the group.

Ahaan: {thinking} If she leaves the group, I'll be all alone. It's not like others don't treat me well, but everyone is Hella scared of me. I wonder why every time my favorite person leaves me. First Mom and now her!

As they reached home everyone was enjoying themselves, Alishka went to her room and Ahaan joined Maanvir in cleaning the equipment. Although Maanvir was scared of Ahaan but also had brotherhood for him and seeing him a little tensed and sad, he finally asked if everything was fine? Ahaan just nodded his head.

Saina: Oh Ahaan, when did you guys arrive? Where's Alishka?

Ahaan: We just arrived a little while ago. Alishka is in her room right now.

Saina: Okay, could you call Alishka? It's already time for evening tea. I'll go make it.!

Maanvir: Dude, if it had been masala Maggi, it would've been so much more fun!

Adhiraj: {joining in} Why not Alishka's special one?

Ahaan: Yeah, why not. {whispering} Just one last time!

Maanvir: but someone call her.

Himanshu: Alishkaaaaaa, come quickly! Today, we'll have your special homemade masala Maggi!

Saina: Alishkaaaaaa, I am making the tea. Come here before that!

Alishka: {from a far} OKKKK! GIVE ME 5 MINS

Alishka came down wearing a normal attire with a messy bun and entered the kitchen where Saina was already there making tea for everyone. She passed a warm smile to Alishka, to which she smiled back but weakly. Alishka made her special Masala Maggie and served it everyone.

Maanvir: {licking his fingers} Mmm, so tasty, Alishka, your recipe is our lifeline! I don't know when we'll get to eat like this again after you leave.

Hearing this Alishka looked at him with shock. Ahaan elbowed her to finally tell the truth. Maanvir just looked at her with a little smirk, expect him everyone was confused.

Alishka: {hesitatingly}guys.... I can't do Paranormal investigating anymore; I have got a job offer from a company.

Saina: Wait what?

Chapter 5

Himanshu: Guys, if this is a joke, please stop right there!

Adhiraj: I feel like it's a hundred percent a joke!

Saina: Alishka what's the real matter?

Alishka explained them everything, everyone sitting there was either devastated or shocked to hear that.

Maanvir: I also feel like quitting all this now, not just Alishka!

Adhiraj: Dude, are you guys out of your minds?

Ahaan: It's not our minds, it's our luck that's bad!

Himanshu: We can understand Alisha's issue, but what's your take Maanvir? Why you want to quit?

Maanvir: It's the same old financial struggle! Think about it, it's been 3 years, but we're still in the same 3 BHK flat! We're still driving the same Vitara Brezza that we bought with our first income, still doing the same things we used to do in college! If we find someone like Mr. Singhania, we get good payment, but if we find someone else, it's low payment! Guys, just tell me one thing, our parents didn't educate us to live like this!

Saina: Vir, wasn't this our dream?

Adhiraj: So, if we're not able to live a comfortable life, you'll give all this up?

Ahaan: Yes! True, we may not have a lot of money, a fancy house, or a luxury car, but at least we have this friendship! We're always together, having fun, supporting each other, and most importantly, we are happy and not stressed or depressed due to workload. And still, you want to switch to that life.

Maanvir: Oh really? And what about our parents? Actually, I should say grandparents. You see, with the little we earn, we manage our expenses. But now, they're getting older, and it's our responsibility to take care of them. With such limited funds, it's either we take care of them or ourselves!

Alishka: Guys, if my mom was okay, I would never ever think of leaving. But understand this is my compulsion or perhaps it's just the destiny that our journey together had to end here.

Himanshu: Maanvir, if you've thought about quitting, then you must have received a job offer too, right?

Maanvir: Not just me, Saina, a job offer has come for you too!

Saina: {narrowing her eyebrows} wait what?

Maanvir: Guys, I've received a job offer as a manager from Ahaan's dad's company, and Saina, you've also received an appointment letter as a history teacher at Global Sunrise School.

Adhiraj: so, its final That we are disbanding the group?

EVERYONE: YES!

Ahaan: this was bound to happen one day but not today.

Adhiraj: are you guys serious? I mean......

Himanshu: {interrupting} Bhai, I just applied for a letter for membership in a major paranormal investigating team in the USA. This might be our future now!

Saina: Guys today is our last day together! Let's enjoy it. One last time, all together?

Alishka: I agree.

Everyone enjoyed there last days by watching movies playing video games and doing their fun activities together.

The next morning everyone started shifting, Alishka and Saina shared room together as well as Adhiraj and Himanshu and Ahaan and Maanvir. They were all engrossed in some or other work. Alishka and Saina were taking out the wall hangings, photographs, paintings, and etc. Ahaan and Maanvir were taking out the furniture's, some of them were to be sold and some of them were going into Maanvir's new apartment given to him by the company, Adhiraj was typing a closing letter to all sites so that there are no more appointments coming to them. Himanshu was also engrossed with shifting. Alishka was taking out some pictures from the wall, but her eyes stood at one picture it was a photograph of them all.

She was feeling a lot of guilt and there was a heavy feeling on her chest. This wasn't the first trauma she got this year but was three in a row. Saina saw her staring at the picture, she came, and side hugged her. Seeing the girls everyone came near them as it was the last thing to get out of the flat, as all the flat was empty. Everyone became emotional after seeing that picture frame. They all shared a warm hug and took out the picture.

Maanvir: Come on, brothers and sister, if destiny wills it, we'll definitely meet again!

Alishka: {whispering to herself} Destiny isn't favoring our togetherness at all!!!

Adhiraj: Himanshu what's the timing of flights.

Himanshu: Bhai it's of 4 clocks.

Saina: Wait a minute, did you guys finalize joining that paranormal team?

Adhiraj: Exactly, why wouldn't they want capable officers like us?

Himanshu: By the way, Saina, we're all going to miss you. Even though you're Maanvir's girlfriend, we've mostly gone on missions together. I hope we find a partner like you.

Adhiraj: Exactly!

Saina: {keeping her hand on both of their Sholders} ofc you will get for sure.

Maanvir: {holding both Aliksha and Ahaan by the shoulders} The three of you were our perfect trio!

Alishka: yes beautiful! If my life was a novel, time spent with you guys will be my favorite chapter!

Saina: Oh yes, Shakespeare's sister, just don't forget me, although you've almost forgotten me after getting together with Ahaan, but still, do call me, okay?

Alishka: {slightly slapping her on the shoulder} Are you crazy? As if you haven't forgotten after Vir bhai's arrival!

Both girls hugged each other tightly. Ahaan was standing quietly and staring Alishka Lost in his own pool of thought, Maanvir patted his Sholder bringing back from his trance.

Maanvir: Ahaan, don't you think you're forgetting something too?

Ahaan: Guys....... I know.... That I am a very cold person.. ....and I have scared you a lot....... but trust that was never my intention....... it's just a personality trait......I got from my father.... but trust me I love you all....... And will never hurt you.

Everyone: its ok yarr

Everyone shared a group hug and went to their own respective house. Maanvir and Saina moved in together. Adhiraj went back to his parents and told them everything and eventually got the permission to go to USA for the job as his elder brother supported him. Same situation happened at Himanshu's house but eventually after small fights and emotional blackmail his mother and sister gave him the permission. Here at Alishka's house, she was packing her things and her having chat with her father, although she was very disappointed of what her father did but still, she chose to remain silent as Afterall it was the question of her mother's life. She was almost done, but suddenly something clicked her mind and went towards her bed drawers and took out an album in which there were Polaroid of her childhood pictures, school time, college time and lastly pictures of her favorite time. She was going through all of them, all the flashbacks and memories were covering her head and suddenly her eyes fell on a cute picture of her and Ahaan in high school. In an instant, the doorbell chimed, prompting her father to investigate while Alishka found herself drifting into a reverie of memories.

There was weak smile in her lips, suddenly her room door opened it was Ahaan who just came to bid her Farwell Afterall she was the only person who cared about him and was his comfort place. Seeing Alishka lost in some picture he went near her and had a smile in his face when he saw the picture. This picture contained a lot of emotions and memories. Both were looking still at the picture when her dad interrupted by calling out her name from outside the room.

Alishka: {jolting} coming Dad.

Ahaan: {smirk} seem like someone's going to miss me.

Alishka: {startled} Huh when did you arrive?

Ahaan helped her to get down the luggage and waited for her in the car. Alishka hugged her dad and said goodbye. They then first went to the hospital and met her mom and then to the airport. On the other hand, Adhiraj and Himanshu too came to the airport as they didn't get any straight flight to USA and now had to go via Delhi, so they and Alishka were sharing same flight. Although the whole time Alishka had a smile on her face but still fear of losing her mother was making her go insane. Everyone reached the airport, and it was an hour before the flight everyone was talking except Alishka every time her thoughts were taking her towards her mother's pale face. Her intrusive thoughts were making her mad, thoughts like what if it's the last time she was seeing her mom. What if something happens to her when she is gone? What if her job is not success? What if she couldn't save her mom? All these questions were eating her from inside, her hands were shaking. And wearing a forced smile weighed heavily on her. Ahaan while chatting with others casually glanced at her, seating directly in front of him, he could see line of tension on her forehead and her hands shaking, fingers fidgeting and legs shaking. He became worried seeing her in this condition and tried calling her few times, but she was engulfed in a whirlwind of thoughts and her eyes were fixed on a distant point, unfocused. Ahaan got up and held Alishka's wrist with a tender yet firm grasp. His gentle yet firm hold startled her, bringing back to reality.

Alishka: {staggering} Ahaan? What are you doing? Let go.

Ahaan: {firmly} One moment, let's step aside, I need to talk.

This drew everyone's gaze. Everyone was taken Aback by the sight.

Adhiraj: Oh, so finally, a proposal today? YES!!!

Hearing this, he shot him an angry glare. He dragged her towards a secluded corner.

Alishka: Dude, are you crazy? Why did you pull me over here?

Ahaan: First, you tell me, what's going on?

Alishka: It's nothing, I'm fine!

Ahaan: {staring directly in her eyes} ARE YOU SURE?

Alishka: {deep sigh} It's nothing, buddy, I'm just really worried about Mom!

Ahaan: {reassuring} Alishu, don't worry! I'm here, I'll take care of her completely and I'll update you every day. I promise, I'm serious. And you know that they are like my own parents?

Listening to this, she embraced him tightly, as if she never wanted to let go. His embrace tightened even more, his fingers tenderly tracing patterns through her hair. Reluctantly they released each other from their embrace.

Alishka: {sour voice} Thank you so much Ahaan but promise me if anything goes wrong or if.... if... she leaves me you're going to tell me the truth then and there, no matter what the condition is!

Ahaan: {deep sigh} Fine! I promise. And one more thing.

He tenderly clasped her hand in his, offering her a wristwatch with a soft smile.

Ahaan: Whenever you feel lonely just look at this watch and remember you have me.

Alishka: {warm smile} Thankyou Ahaan you're the best!

Ahaan: Feeling better? Always smile like that, ok? now let's go back.

Alishka: But before that. {She retrieved her wristwatch from her hand and passed it to him.} I want you to take this in my memory as I won't be the same after am gone.

He accepted it graciously and enveloped her in another embrace, his smile radiating warmth. they came back and found everyone talking and enjoying their time, they too joined and enjoyed their moments together. Finally, it was the time for flight. Adhiraj and Himanshu hugged everyone and waved goodbye, Aliksha did the same, she became a little emotional, Ahaan flashed her a reassuring smile, conveying that everything would be alright. Then they all left for flight, Ahaan stood there watching her disappear in the crowd. A realization dawned on him that things wouldn't be the same with Alishka in the future, and he also wouldn't be the same after their meeting. He understood how deeply he cared for her, yet the inability to help her, despite his wealth, shattered him from within. Glancing at the wristwatch she had given him, he clutched it tightly, bringing it close to his heart.

After that everyone went their separate ways, Maanvir became Manager at Ahaan's dad's company, Ahaan took over the business and became the CEO of company, Saina became history teacher at a well-known school, Adhiraj and Himanshu joined one of the best paranormal investigating team and came into limelight, in USA everyone knew about them, Alishka became manager at INDIA BASKET {fictional}. They were all leading a normal life.

Chapter 6

It's been two years since the disband, everyone was busy with their own life, they were successful and were living a wealthy life. Maanvir and Saina grew more in love with each other. Himanshu and Adhiraj were still good friends in fact they were leading the life of their dreams. They were known as International Paranormal investigators; they shot in many shows and were a part of huge paranormal society. Ahaan was always focused during his work but as time passed, he became more outgoing and jollier in nature. Maanvir and Ahaan eventually became good friends as they worked at the same company. Alishka made efforts to overcome her trauma, but isolation from her family and friends caused her to become introverted and distant.

"Please, please let me go. What did I do to you?" pleaded a girl.

"The one who falls into MY TRAP never survives! HA-HAHAHA!" said a devil woman, laughing evilly.

"Then WHY DON'T YOU KILL ME!! WHY HAVE YOU IMPRISONED ME HERE IN THESE SHACKLES??"

"BECAUSE IF I KILL YOU AND YOUR SISTER, I WILL BE FREE, AND THEN... HAHAHAHA, THIS WITCH WILL RULE THE WORLD! CALL ALEENA, BRING ALISHKA HERE NOWWW!"

"NOOO! YOU WON'T DO ANYTHING TO HER, I'D RATHER DIE MYSELF BUT IF ANYTHING HAPPENS TO MY FAMILY... AAAAHHH NO, LET ME GO AAAAAAAHHHHH."

The devil Erupted in fury and began thrashing with a lash. In a voice seething in anger, she said.

"CALL HER, CALL HER, OTHERWISE YOU'LL KEEP SUFFERING!"

In a tearful tone, she begged her stop.

"NO LET ME GOO"

"Call her, call herrrrr!!!"

"ALISHKAAAAAAAA!!!! ALISHKAAAAA!!"

Here Alishka was fast asleep exhausted from the events of the day. When Aleena {her sister's} voice caught her attention. She began experiencing same nightmare that used to haunt her every day. She started shaking and struggled to rise, but her efforts were in vain. After numerous efforts, she finally woke up from that terrible nightmare. She rose, grasping for breath, her entire body drenched in sweat and tears streaming from her eyes. She got out of bed and headed to the kitchen for some water to cool down. Suddenly a notification popped up on her phone, she checked it, to her surprise, it was pdf about vacation planning and related information. As she was reading, she received a call from her friend, and she felt a bit strange.

Himanshu: Hello Alishka? I hope I didn't disturb u.

Alishka: {rubbing her eyes} No, no you didn't. but is everything ok? I mean calling so late.

Himanshu: yes, did you open the pdf?

Alishka: {raising her brow} Yeah... but a free vacation? I mean, I hope you're not caught up in some scam?

Himanshu: Oh no, not at all! Actually, I was booking a ticket for my cousin on liveyourtrip.com, and then this offer popped up. You know it's a trusted site, right? So, yeah, I thought why not give it a try, and fortunately, we won a free voucher.

Alishka: Intelligent and lucky. Proud of you bhai!

Himanshu: Thanks, I'll inform everyone about it. Until then, you take care of the leaves. Me and Adi are coming to India tomorrow itself.

Alishka: Okay, wait! Are all six of us involved in this?

Himanshu: Yeah, I mean I've included everyone {teasing tone}, it's just that Ahaan might refuse, you know?

Alishka: Why would he refuse? And if he does, let him know, I'm coming too...

Adhiraj: {interrupting} Yeah, then he'll come running on one leg!

Alishka: {irritated} Yeah, that's what was missing, you!

Adhiraj: Hi Alisha! How are you? You never call Haan?

Alishka: hello! I am fine. Sorry busy life. I will meet you guys soon till bye and goodnight.

Saying that she hung up the phone, she glanced at the clock and realized it was morning already. She yawned, then opened her laptop to draft a two week leave application.

Meanwhile Adi and Himanshu informed and explained everything to everyone and prepared for the trip.

Everyone was happy and excited to meet each other a long time. Saina Called Aliksha and they talked about the trip, clothes, event. Himanshu explained everything to everyone about the place, hotel sites and activities they were going to do there.

Alishka came back to Mumbai four days early to visit her parents and relax before the trip.

Everyone made their preparation for the trip, and there was palpable excitement as they looked forward to reuniting after such a long time.

CHAPTER 7

Maanvir and Ahaan looking each other with guilt.

Saina: {frustrated} You two always keep us waiting!

Saina: When I said to go to bed early, what did you say? {mimicking Maanvir} Just 10 more minutes, Sannu!

Ahaan: Well, sis-in-law, it happens, at least we're going to reach the airport.

Maanvir: Sannu don't get angry before the trip; it will spoil the trip!

Saina: You know how excited I am to meet Alisha and these two pranksters?

Maanvir: Okay, sorry baba. Look, we're at the airport now. Let's calm down, okay?

After settling the bill, they proceeded to the airport. Here in airport Adi and Himanshu were already waiting and as soon as they spotted them, they rushed over, wrapping each other in light, heartfelt embraces. Everyone had gathered except her, which left him feeling anxious.

Ahaan: {Anxious} Guys, we're all here. Where's Alisha?

Saina: {squinting her eyebrows} Haan where is she?

Himanshu: {with a smirk} there she is.

Saying this he gestured towards her, prompting everyone to turn around and catch sight of her. As Saina saw her, she screamed with excitement, then rushed over to her enveloping her in a tight hug. They shared a warm embrace before releasing each other, then clasped hands and hurried towards the rest of the group. She met everyone. Upon the eye contact of Ahaan and Aliksha they shook hands although wanted to hug each other really bad but they didn't do anything like that Infront of group.

Maanvir: all thanks to Himanshu who made this reuniting possible.

Ahaan: Exactly, buddy. Remember, two years ago we all came to say goodbye to each other, and today we're meeting again!

Alishka: {shocked} Ahaan, you've changed a lot!

Adhiraj: Yeah, I mean when I came to hug him, I thought I'd get a death glare, but instead, I got a warm smile.

Saina: Well, he's changed a lot from being with us all this time!

Himanshu: So, we don't need to be scared, right?

Ahaan: {smirking} Yeah, just don't interfere with my work, I can handle the rest of the craziness!

Alishka: wow......{whispering} good for you!

Ahaan: {whispering back} good for u too.

Alishka just ignored his words; she took Saina with her and went towards the cafeteria to grab something.

Ahaan: {scratching his head} Dude what's the matter with Alisha.

Himanshu: {smirking} Oh, worries, huh?

Ahaan: That's bound to happen, guys. In fact, it shouldn't just be me, but all of us! While we all had someone with us... but she was alone there. I hope she hasn't changed.

Adhiraj: Yeah, that's true. No one's alone this time; we're all together for two weeks, at least. We'll make it right!

But Ahaan wasn't feeling good he was thrilled at the prospect of their reunion after such a long time. However, her subbed response left him feeling somewhat melancholy. While everyone else was engaged in conversation, he quietly observed her, eagerly awaiting an opportunity to speak with her privately. Finally, when he spotted her walking alone, he hurriedly approached her to strike up a conversation.

Ahaan: {tapping her back} hey?

Alishka: {jolting a bit} Oh hey!

Ahaan: Why are you ignoring me?

Alishka: No, it's not like that.

Ahaan: hmm. and how are you?

Alishka: {dryly} fine! What about you?

Ahaan: {narrowing his eyebrows} your everything but fine!

Alishka: well, I can't hide anything from you!

She confided in him about her worries, leading to a meaningful and cathartic conversation between them. He listened attentively to everything she had to say, absorbing each word with care. After hearing her out, he comforted her, lifting her spirits and bringing a sense of relief and happiness to her. There was finally a sense of relief and understanding between them. A genuine smile graced her face as she side-hugged him, feeling a sense of readiness for the journey ahead. They regrouped and settled in, anticipating their upcoming flight.

Adhiraj: Guys, this is our first ever trip in which we won't be experiencing anything paranormal, or you can say a trip without anything paranormal, right?

Saina: I agree, finally we all are going on a normal trip!

Ahaan: {smirking} Well our last experiences doesn't allow us to think like that!

Maanvir: yes, this trip might be containing any UNKNOWN ADVENTURE.

Alishka: Hey what's the name of the place, I don't know why I have heard its name somewhere.

Saina: Guys, what's the name of this place? It's quite confusing.

Ahaan: ALANCHAL

Chapter 8

Everyone was asleep in the flight except for Ahaan engrossed in his laptop working. They all were travelling in business class. Alishka was peacefully sleeping when suddenly she heard someone whispering her name.

'ALIISHKAAAA..........'

"Alishka................."

Alishka: {sleep talking} huh who?

Ahaan who was sitting beside her caught her sleep talking. He glanced at her confused. Alishka abruptly woke up, grasping for breath. Ahaan was completely bewildered by what had just occurred.

Ahaan: {patting her back} hey are you ok?

Alishka: huh? Were you calling my name?

He shook his head and passed her a glass of water. After that an announcement was made that they will be landing soon. The flight landed and everyone proceeded to retrieve their luggage from the baggage claim area. Upon stepping out of the airport, they felt a noticeable drop in temperature, accompanied by a chill in the air. Everyone grabbed a warm sweater or jacket to wear, ensuring that nobody caught a cold.

Saina: {shaking voice} So.... Guys.... What's.... next?

Himanshu: {reading} Mr. timber?

Everyone: what?

Adhiraj: Oh, that's our driver's name. After a 5-hour flight, we also have a two-hour road trip ahead!

Maanvir: {holding his head} Guys, what's this? A two-hour road trip. Just hearing it makes me dizzy!

Alishka: And by the way, if we've reached Alanchal, then why do we have a 2-hour journey left?

Himanshu: Guys, Alanchal is just a small hill station with only one waterfall worth visiting, but through the offer we've got, we're being taken to a really nice resort where there are plenty of fun activities like rock climbing, bungee jumping, trekking available. Moreover, there are many places similar to ours nearby, that's why.

Saina: SMART

Maanvir: But why a 2-hour road trip?

Ahaan: Come on, what's the problem with a road trip, buddy? We'll enjoy seeing the beautiful landscapes, the beauty of nature, different trees, and flowers along the way. It'll be fun, don't be such a bore.

Adhiraj: {pointing}. Sir over here

They loaded their luggage and settled into their seats accordingly. Maanvir was so exhausted that he chose the back seat, plugged in his earphone and drifted off to sleep, so did Adhiraj, Himanshu sat on the front seat guiding the driver as he had all the details, Saina, Alishka and Ahaan were sitting in the middle seat. During the drive, Ahaan gazed at the passing scenery and enjoyed the view of nature outside. He smiled at the view and took it all in, feeling a sense of peace and contentment. Alishka had been observing him since they met and was confused and shocked to see this significant change in his personality and behavior. A person who was typically reserved, introverted, and rarely smiled or spoke much, underwent a surprising change into someone who loves traveling, going out, and smiles frequently. Observing this, she felt happy for him but also a twinge of sadness about herself, realizing how she had let herself go completely over the past few years.

Saina: Hey Alisha listen!

Alishka: yes?

Saina: {showing her pictures} Which dress should I wear for tonight's dinner?

Alishka: The red frock will be fine! But wait, is there any special occasion today?

Ahaan: {interrupting} Hey, wasn't it mentioned in the trip manual that there's going to be a dinner party today as it's the hotel's golden jubilee.

Alishka: oh yes! I completely forgot about that.

Saina: Did you not bring any casual or partywear attire?

Alishka: No, Yaar. But its okay, you guys enjoy. I'll stay in and sleep.

Maanvir: What's up, Alishka? So, what if you don't have partywear clothes? You have to join us in the party.

Himanshu: And what else, Alishka ji? You're getting a free buffet, and you want to sleep?

Ahaan: Haan Alishu you have to come!

Alishka: {palming her head} ok fine!

after 2 hours of journey

Himanshu: OK! guys we're here.

"As he uttered those words, everyone glanced out of the car window and beheld a magnificent resort. It was grand, adorned with vibrant colors, beautiful windows, a large fountain, and an imposing gate."

"They were mesmerized by its architecture, marveling at how beautifully it was constructed on the slope, featuring small windows and balconies that adorned its façade."

"They were baffled by how quickly they completed their two-hour road trip and arrived at the hotel. Upon their arrival, they were greeted warmly by the staff. Four members promptly assisted with their luggage, guiding them to their VIP suite, while two others escorted them to lunch. The expansive buffet, offering a wide array of food choices, lifted their spirits. Following a satisfying meal, another staff member escorted them to their suites. They were all astonished by the beauty of their accommodations. Expressing their gratitude for the excellent booking, they retired to their rooms to rest."

CHAPTER 9

It was 7 in the evening everyone was sleeping comfily inside their blankets with heaters on. Ahaan woke up got down from the bed switched off the heater, stretched his hands and head a bit. He went and opened his suitcase and took out a white paper bag with a dress in it. After that he came out of his room and was just closing the door when someone called from a far.

Adhiraj: Oh Mr. Agni dev?

Ahaan: what now?

Adhiraj: Bro, aren't you feeling cold? It's zero degrees here! And you're wearing just a t-shirt and Bermuda shorts!

Listening to this he realized that he was wearing less clothes according to the weather, not wanting to catch cold he went in wore sweater and jackets and then came out.

Adhiraj: Bro, what's the rush? We still have time for dinner!

Ahaan: abe sab so rahe hain kya?{ is everyone sleeping?}

Maanvir: {from behind} Nope Sir!

Ahaan: Well, where Alisha's room?

Himanshu: The last one in the lobby, by the way, what's the gift?

He ignored his words and went towards her room. He tried knocking but the door was already opened, he entered the room that was dark pitch black there was only a little streetlight coming inside from the window near the couch. He entered the room with sleek footsteps thinking that she is asleep. Unaware

Alishka: Ahaan?

Ahaan: {almost tripping} AAAAAAAA! Alishka!!!! Are you out of your mind?

Ahaan: {scanning the room} Where are you though?

Alishka: Open the lights u will find me!

Feeling a little weird he searched for the switches and finally switched on the lights and saw her standing near the window and gazing outside. She gestured him come near through her hands. He went and stood a little far from her. He was facing her back.

Alishka: {in a weird tone} Look at these trees, it feels like they've been strategically placed here!

Ahaan: {confused} Yeah, it's a bit strange but...

Alishka: If we cut down these trees, it will be better!

Ahaan: {narrowing his eyebrow} Hey? Are you ok?

Saina was sleeping peacefully when someone started calling her name. she couldn't open her eyes but felt as if some energy was asking for help.

"Sainaaaaaaaaa!!! Please help, she's going to kill him!!!!!!"

Saina: {hushed voice} who are you?

"Alishkaaaaaa, it's me, Alishka! She has taken control of my body! Please, Ahaan is with her, save him."

Listening her name Saina woke up abruptly she could not see her but felt her presence, Maanvir came out of bathroom and started sensing a strong energy around him, he saw Saina breathing heavily and her eyes open wide.

Saina: {shouting} Maanvir! AHAAN'S LIFE IS IN DANGER!

Here Adhiraj was unpacking when he started hearing his Electromagnetic Field Meter {description given above} started beeping. His eyes were in shock, he looked at Himanshu who was at staring at him with same shock. Alishka looked at Ahaan with big eyes and weird smile, she tilted her head sidewards and walked towards him in a horrible way.

Ahaan: {sensing} Alishka? You're.........

Saina: Ahaan! MOVE AWAY FROM HER, SHE'S POSSESSED BY A DEMON!

Ahaan heard this scream coming from outside, he turned his face towards the door, Maanvir and Saina pushed the door and entered the room. Ahaan was all confused looking at their expression and looked back at Alishka who was standing really close to him without any gap. as he looked at her again, Alishka pushed Ahaan with a strength she never had, it felt like suddenly she got a strength of bodybuilder. Ahaan was in air and was going to collide with Mirror and hurt himself badly an unknown energy lifted him and threw him towards the bed.

Saina: {approaching and holding her head} WHO ARE YOU? WHAT DO YOU WANT?

Devil: {ALISHAS BODY} HER SOUL.

Saina: LET GO OF MY FRIEND OR ELSE IT WON'T END WELL FOR YOU!!!!

Devil: {laughing} I DIDN'T LET GO OF HER SISTER, WHY WOULD I LET GO OF HER?

Ahaan: {fuming in anger} WHOEVER YOU ARE! RELEASE HER BODY IMMEDIATELY OR YOU'LL FACE THE WORST FROM ME!

Dayan looked at him and smiled weirdly.

Devil: WHEN ALEENA'S LOVER COULDN'T SAVE HER, HOW WILL YOU SAVE?

Himanshu: GUYS, WE NEED TO ACT FAST! THE INFRARED THERMOMETER IS SHOWING THAT HER TEMPERATURE IS DROPPING EVERY SECOND! WE ARE LOSING ALISHKA.

Saina: WHO ARE YOU AAAAAAA!!!! GUYS I CAN'T FOCUS!!!!!!!

Devil: NO ONE CAN DO ANYTHING! AHAAN, IT'S TIME TO SAY GOODBYE TO ALISHKA!

Ahaan: SAINA? PLZ TACKLE HER FOR MINUTES.

Adhiraj: THIS SITUATION HAS NEVER COME BEFORE. CAN WE SAVE ALISHKA?

Ahaan returned with a copper bottle with him, he slides opened the bottle threw all the water over Alisha's body. As the Devil felt water she started to scream loudly, she pushed Saina to the ground and started screaming in a terrible manner she rose up in air and a black smoke started coming out her mouth, Alishka body was a spinning slowly in the Air. Everyone was taken aback from this site. That smoke escaped by breaking window glass. As all the smoke escaped her body, her body became lifeless and fragile, she was going to fall, but Ahaan caught her in the middle saving her from a terrible accident. Alishka laid lifeless in his arms, panicking he checked his hand for pulse and luckily, she was still alive. Her body was drenched with water but was burning from fever.

Ahaan: Guys, Alishu has a very high fever!! This means?

Saina: she stills has control over her body.

Maanvir: We need to save Alishka.

Adhiraj: we don't have any knowledge about it.

Suddenly Saina heard a whisper: I won't leave her.

Saina: {trembling} guys we need act in time.

It was a chain tension, firstly the attack and second this. Everyone was panicking at this.

Ahaan: But but the spirit has left her body, right? Then how?

Maanvir: Himanshu, Adi, have you guys continued with the paranormal investigations? You should know, right?

Saina: Although the evil spirit left the body, but it still has its control over her.

They were already in shock after witnessing what just happened. Himanshu took out his phone and started searching about it.

Ahaan: {gritting his teeth} guys we're wasting our time.

Saina: we're losing her!!

Himanshu: MAHAMATI AASHRAM!!

Everyone just looked at him with uncertainty.

Chapter 10

Ahaan: Meaning?

Himanshu: Here in Alanchal, there is a very large ashram of saints where people go for peace of mind. It's a place known for its peace and solidarity, moreover, it's an ashram connected with a temple, a place where God resides. I think they can help us now!

Adhiraj: Yes, that's a valid point. If we want to save Alishka, let's head there!

Saina: First, all of you go outside and I'll change her clothes! Adi, please inform the hotel about the broken window!!

Ahaan: No! The water I poured on her is from the Ganges! Once it dries, the demon won't be able to attack her again!

Adhiraj: Guys, the ashram is within walking distance from here. Let's take her there, but first, Ahaan, put this Om necklace around her neck! After that, the demon won't be able to attack her!

Ahaan took that necklace from Adhiraj and placed it in her neck, then they called for a Cab from hotel reception and luckily found one. They took her to that ashram. As they entered the place where it was situated, they were mesmerized by its beauty. The ashram was bustling with activity: cows, saints, and women saints were either praying or lighting up the diyas. They stopped the cab right in front of the main gate. They saw three ladies standing in front of the gate, waiting for them. One of them was an elderly lady, radiating an aura of wisdom and divinity. Adhiraj and Himanshu got out of the car and talked to them, explaining the whole situation. After a while Adhiraj gestured, Ahaan to bring out Alishka He stepped out of the car, cradling her in his arms, ready to enter. However, the elderly lady interrupted him.

Pujaran: {broad eyes} Stop right there!

She whispered something into the ears of a girl standing near her and the girl nodded she clapped her hand twice. Four women carrying a wooden folding came and laid Aliksha and tied her body with a red cloth to it. Then they picked up the folding and went away, after that the lady gestured everyone to come.

Ahaan: where did they take her?

Pujaran: Where she will find peace and purity!

Everyone went in and were made to sit in an office.

Himanshu: How did you know, Maa ji? That we would come?

Pujaran: When you set foot in Alanchal, my son, I knew that you would come here for sure.

Adhiraj: Maa ji who are you and this aashram?

Pujaran: {sleek smile} This ashram belongs to me. My father opened this ashram in 1800, which is for those who are unhappy with their lives or struggling with life. He had many wonderful mental powers, so people who faced spiritual issues also came here.

Saina: Maa ji, does Alishka have any connection to this place?

Pujaran: YES!

Chapter 11

The billowing smoke transformed into a female demon, possessing a corpulent form, crimson eyes, and a slender nose.

Aleena lay there like a living corpse, frail and pallid, with bruises marring her body, bound in shackles. The demon scowled at her, unleashing a torrent of anger and distress through vehement shouts.

Aleena: STOP IT!! STOP IT!!!!

Dayan: How did she defeat me in the end? Dravilla? No, now Alishka and everyone will die! HAHAHAHAH!

Saina: Maa ji, me and Alishka.......

Pujaran: (interrupting) I know you both are sensitive! But there is another power within you that is the fierce form of this power!

Maanvir: Maa ji, will our Alishka be saved? She's enduring a lot! First her sister's departure...

Pujaran: HER sister is alive!

Himanshu: JI? {what}

Pujaran: You don't want to know why this is happening to Alishka after all?

Ahaan: I want to know!

Pujaran: You care deeply for her! If this journey is successful, you two will find each other's company.

Ahaan: Maa Ji, could you please tell us what has been troubling her all this time?

Saina: And how did that spirit enter her body?

Pujaran: 'astral projection' Ever heard about?

Saina: the ability of a person's spirit to travel to distant places.

Pujaran: You're quite insightful! Yes, with this power, we can gain control over our dreams and even leave our bodies to observe them. Perhaps, one night, Alishka unintentionally left her body while sleeping, and that's when Dravilla seized control of her body!

Adhiraj: {squinting his eyebrows} Maa ji? Could this be the same witch from the 90s who was Known for her dark magic? Wasn't she sealed away by a great sage in a cave?

Pujaran: Drithi and Dravilla... Meaning me and my twin sister. We were both daughters of the head priest of this Ashram. We were like Lakshmi and Alakshmi. While I was walking on the path of worship, righteousness, understanding scriptures, and goodness, my sister Dravilla was fond of dark magic, worshiping demons since childhood.

And she had the power to influence minds since childhood, what you call 'persuasion' in your language. At first, Father never found out about her, while I knew that she was practicing Black Magic and dark forces were gradually entering her. Then one day Father saw her performing animal sacrifice and practicing black magic, he severely beat her and locked her in a room where she screamed and shouted... and the next day her body was found in that room, there was a lot of black water under her body, Father called some Aghoris and performed her last rites. My father thought that a severe crisis would come... and it did Because this ashram is a place of God, so her soul had to leave here immediately, but I don't know from where she got many black magical powers and started killing innocent people... and she didn't spare my mother either... Then Father, along with many priests, performed a very big ritual and managed to control her and we imprisoned her in a cave.

Ahaan: But Maa ji? What connection does she have with Alishka? And has anyone set her free?

Pujaran: Yes, Aleena! She's the one who set her free.

Saina: Aleena? But why would she do such a thing?

Maanvir: hatred, jealousy and yes evil too.

Saina: {sync with Adhiraj and Himanshu} what?

Ahaan: Yes, Aleena despised Alishka! I know how she treated her! That's why I always hated her from the start.

Adhiraj: But why?

Ahaan: {smiling} you guys call her your friend? Anyways, Aleena hatted Alishka throughout her entire life, just because of her ability, talents and love that she received from elders, parents and teachers. Although Alishka tried to makeup with her sister but always failed. Moreover, Alisha's parents Always criticized her for no doing well and cursed her a lot which made her hatred grow deeper for Aliksha.

Saina: Listen, I knew that her sister is rude, but this is the scene? Aleena will go till this extent. I think we shouldn't save her.

Pujaran: Only Alishka will tell! What you should do next. Either fight against that witch and save this town or save your own life and leave!!

Himanshu: this place needs us?

Pujaran: yes and no

Maanvir: {crossing his hand} meaning?

Pujaran: {deep sigh} It means it's up to you! This town needs to be saved. But it's your choice whether you want to save it or not?

Maanvir: And if we declined? Wont you stop us?

Pujaran: {sleek smile} No, because we have full faith that someday, some brave warriors will surely come to save us!

As they were talking a girl entered the room and whispered something into her ear. Her eyes went wide, and she stood up with the help of a stick, seeing her everyone present there stood up too.

Pujaran: {raising her voice} YOU CAN MEET ALISHKA! NOW SHE IS ABSOLUTELY FINE!

Adhiraj: BUT MAA JI? WHAT HAPPENED?

Girl: {who just entered} A spirit has entered our Ashram!

Saina: {taking a long deep breath} Yes, I can feel it!

Suddenly, the room plunged into darkness, enveloped in an eerie silence as a chill swept through the air. Then, out of nowhere, a piercing scream shattered the stillness. That scream sent shivers down everyone's spines, causing her to tremble uncontrollably and collapse to the ground in fear.

CHAPTER 12

Girl: {shivering} MAA JI, what should we do??

Pujaran: {quavering and deep} A grave danger has arrived!

Saina: {showing her finger} Ruko! I can contact her! Adi? Do you still have that Spirit Box?

Adhiraj: Nahi but still through your ability you can contact her, Remember?

Saina: {fidgeting} Am not sure about it; it's been 2 years!

Pujaran: {deep voice} Keep full faith in yourself! Your strength is even greater than this!

"Her profound words penetrated deep into her consciousness, plunging her into a contemplative state where she endeavoured to communicate solely through her thoughts."

She knelt, focusing her mind on silence, attempting to connect with the spirit in the room.

Suddenly, she heard the sorrowful cry of a young girl, a plaintive sound that spoke of pain and a desperate desire to flee.

Saina: WHO ARE YOU AND HOW DID YOU COME HERE?

You can hear me?' a girl replied from a far

Saina: Yes, I can help you.

'Save me please, I need freedom' the girl pleaded

Pujaran: You're Free, Ritu, you can go now

'But Dravilla?'

Saina: SHE WONT BE ABLE TO DO ANYTHING TO YOU!

Suddenly all the lights came, and everything was fine now. Everyone relived but yet shocked. Saina got up and laid down in the nearby sofa and slept immediately.

Himanshu: Saina? What happened to her?

Pujaran: Exhaustion!

Maanvir went towards her, sat near her, tracing his fingers through her hair.

Pujaran: You guys should stay here, or else dravilla can attack you all again.

Adhiraj: Ji maa Ji

Ahaan: Maa ji? Alishka......

Pujaran: you will meet her in the morning!.......{telling some maids} Take these people to athethe {guest} Kaksh{room}.

The servant gestured for them to follow her, and Maanvir picked her up in his arms, carrying her along. The servant escorted them to the guest room and ensured they were comfortable before leaving them to settle in. One of the maids provided them with instructions regarding the rules and timing for dinner. Given that all other rooms were occupied by guests, saints, and other individuals, they were provided with three rooms to accommodate everyone.

Ahaan found himself lost in thought, observing everyone else happily engaged with their partners, which left him feeling alone and melancholic. Her thoughts inundated his mind, nearly overwhelming him with the gravity of what he had just noticed. He longed for a meeting with her, in the hope that it would quiet the troubling thoughts plaguing his mind.

After a while, some attendees brought their dinner to where they were, reassuring them that they would finally meet her tomorrow and that she was doing well. They informed them that she needed rest now, emphasizing that it was imperative not to disturb her tonight as it was essential for her to recharge, as per the saints' orders.

Chapter 13

It was 6am in the morning everyone was sleeping in their room, except Ahaan who couldn't sleep due to his concern for Alishka, all the incidences were flashing in his mind, making him feel somewhat melancholy. He was disturbed by knocking in the door.

Ahaan: {with a jerk} Come in.

Adhiraj: {shaking his hand} hello! Morning.

Ahaan: Adi early morning?

Adhiraj: {jokingly} yes Himan sahib's snores always takes away my sleep

Ahaan: {smiling} You can sleep here if you want to?

Adhiraj: Nope not in the mood, BTW am I right, you didn't sleep last night?

Ahaan: Yeah, couldn't sleep at all!

Adhiraj: {scratching his head} Can I ask something by the way?

Ahaan: {squinting his eyebrows} hmmm?

Adhiraj: Don't get me wrong but, why do you care for her so much? She's just your best friend, isn't she?

Ahaan: {smiling} Well, you tell me, if something ever happens to Himanshu, aren't you worried about him? I'm worried about her That way!

Adhiraj: If I talk about me and Himan, then yes, I care about him, but your case is a little different.

Ahaan: {nodding} I know see the thing is......yes...its true I have feeling for her...but still......our friendship matters most to me.........

Adhiraj: Just because you think, she sees you as a Friend.

Ahaan: Kinda

Over here Alishka was sleeping peacefully in a Room filled with positive energy and rays of morning light, she was roused from her deep sleep by the resonating chimes of the morning prayer bells from the nearby temple. Startled, she snapped awake, her mind and eyes quickly adjusting as she tried to make sense of the sudden awakening. As her eyes acclimated to the surroundings, she was taken aback by the unfamiliarity of her new environment. A sense of fear crept in as she frantically searched for someone familiar. A lady entered the room with a tray of breakfast, noticing her awake. With a warm smile, she helped her rise from the bed and kindly asked about her well-being.

Lady: {warm smile} How are you feeling my dear?

Alishka: {holding her head} A little weak, btw who brought me here? Where am I? What happened to me? Where are my friends?

Lady: Calm down! You'll get answers to all your questions soon, and don't worry, your friends will come to meet you, have your meal first.

Without further argument, Aliksha ate all the breakfast as she was feeling really hungry and weak, after that the lady went away. She got up from the bed and went towards a mirror kept near the bed, as her gaze fell on her body, upon inspecting her body, she realized she was clad in long frock. Shock washed over her as she discovered numerous bruises marring her skin, evidence of some past distress. Frantically scanning her body, she discovered bruises and dark spots covering her hands and shoulders. A scream of pain and trauma escaped her lips as shock and terror overwhelmed her. It felt like a dreadful nightmare she couldn't escape. As her cries echoed through the halls, a group of concerned women swiftly made their way to her room. Inside, they found her trembling on the floor, her head buried between her legs, tears streaming down her cheeks in silent anguish.

Lady: Madam, are you okay?

Alishka: {weeping} Plz call my friends I need them! Please.

Listening to this all the women left her alone; she stood in the same position weeping in trauma of what just happened. All those dark spots marrying her skin, plunged her into deep trauma.

Saina: {knocking} Alishkaaaaaa? May I come in?

Alishka: Saina? Plz come in, I need you.

Saina entered the room, upon seeing Alishka's condition, she hugged her tightly. The embrace offered her immediate solace, but it also unleashed a fresh wave of tears.

Saina: Alishka, calm down now, it's over, you're completely fine now.

Alishka: {breaking the hug} But what happened? Where are we now?

Saina: {comforting} I'll tell you everything, first calm down and sit up, everyone wants to meet you, we're all very worried about you.

Alishka: Is everyone okay now? Are the others fine? Did they not get hurt that day?

Saina: {Agitated} I said everything is fine! Come on, get up, Ahaan is eagerly waiting to meet you!

She assisted her in standing, offering support through her hands, and escorted her outside where her companions eagerly awaited her, ready to provide solace. As everyone saw her coming, they took a sigh of relief and went towards her and asking how was she. Everyone was happy to finally have their Aliksha safe and back. Ahaan was also happy, but his smile faded away as he glanced at the bruises and dark spots on her Sholder and chest. Seeing them made him angry and concerned.

Ahaan: {concerned} Alisha? These stops?

Listening to his words, everybody's attention went towards the spots.

Saina: wait I didn't notice this earlier

Pujaran: {from behind} These are wounds of the fight for freedom! They will heal quickly!

Everyone was a bit startled by her, they turned around to greet her.

Saina: Pranam, Maa ji. Alishka, this is the Pujaran of this place, she saved your life!

Alishka: Pranam maa ji! Thank you for saving my life.

Pujaran: {warm smile} Stay happy. I only did what I had to do, now the rest is up to you!

Alishka: {squinting her eyebrows} ji?

Saina: Alishka, there are many things you need to know! We are ready to help you! But this will be your decision!

Alishka: What decision, what help? Can you please stop speaking in riddles?

Maanvir: Alishka! Before listening to anything, remember that your health is still not well, don't make any decisions hastily!

Alishka: {agitated} Yes! But what's the matter?

Adhiraj: {whispering to Maanvir}: Its better if Ahaan tells her the truth, he will be able to comfort her.

Everyone: Ahaan it's all up to you!

Saying this everyone left the two alone in the corridor. As they found themselves alone, he approached her and embraced her tightly, causing her to be momentarily shocked, but she reciprocated the hug.

Ahaan: {whispering} I thought I lose you that day.

Alishka: You won't get rid of me so easily!

After some time, they reluctantly released from the tight embrace they clasped each other's hands, sharing a warm smile. However, her expression shifted, her smile fading as she gazed at him, her mind swirling with questions.

Ahaan: I know you want answers. I will give them to you! But before that want to go for walk in the nearby garden.

Alishka: {giving in} Fine.

They went outside, in the nearby flower garden. The garden was a picturesque scene, teeming with beautiful wildflowers, trees, butterflies, bees, and birds. The tranquil hum of bees and the melodic chirping of birds filled the air, creating a peaceful ambiance. It was a radiant sunny day, the sky painted in a brilliant shade of blue. Walking through the garden, they were entranced by the mesmerizing sight, feeling a sense of peace wash over their minds as all worries momentarily faded away. She smiled at the enchanting sight, experiencing a profound sense of peace, while he watched her with a smile, finding joy in her happiness. He was delighted to see her in such a healthy state, and he couldn't help but gaze at her throughout their journey, observing her joyful expression as she admired the scenery. But in his mind, a hint of apprehension lingered, as he worried that what he was about to tell her might inadvertently hurt her feelings. A wave of electricity surged through them, causing a chill to run down her spine and prompting her to rub her hands together for warmth. Seeing her discomfort, he swiftly removed his jacket and wrapped it around her shoulders, offering her comfort and warmth. Feeling the warmth of his jacket around her shoulders, she looked towards him with a grateful smile and slipped it on. Spotting a nearby bench, they both decided to take a seat, enjoying the tranquil beauty of the garden together. As they sat and immersed themselves in the garden's beauty, he felt a slight weight on his shoulder, only to discover her resting her head gently against it, her hand wrapped around his.

Ahaan: Beautiful, isn't it?

Alishka: Yeah, finally feeling some peace.

Ahaan: True.

Alishka: Can you tell me now?

Ahaan: Yes, so listen!

As he recounted the story told to them just a day ago, he watched her expression shift from happiness to sadness to sheer trauma. Shock registered on her face as she absorbed every detail. Her mind went numb, and tears welled up in her eyes, overwhelmed by the weight of what she had heard. She swallowed hard, her face draining of color. Suddenly, her world felt turned upside down, and the weight of grief settled heavily on her shoulders, overwhelming her with its burden. She began to breathe heavily, tears streaming down her cheeks, her vision blurring with emotion. Each breath felt like a struggle as she grappled with the overwhelming wave of sorrow. She was in a state of disbelief and deep hurt, struggling to comprehend the enormity of what she had heard. Confusion and trauma gripped her as everything seemed to come to a standstill, enveloping her in a deafening silence where the world around her faded away.

Seeing her in such a state, he enveloped her in his arms, gently guiding her face to rest against his chest, providing her with a safe space to release her pent-up emotions.

Alishka: Plz. tell... me. its... a ...lie

Ahaan: I am sorry, but it's the truth.

Over here Saina and Maanvir were observing them from a little far.

Saina: We weren't even that close when we were just friends!

Maanvir: True that!

Adhiraj: Oh, guys! Stop stalking and please make a decision!

Maanvir: {jolting} Are you mad or what?

Saina: true Adi, you scared us!!

Adhiraj: Achaa sorry sorry! But what now??

Saina: Look, I think we should go to them now. The hugging is over!

Himanshu: By the end of this trip, if these two don't end up like Laila and Majnu...then

Maanvir: {terrified} Oh God, are you two competing to scare us?

Alishka: Guys......

Maanvir: {almost tripping} Oh God... why are you after this kids' lives!

Ahaan: {keeping his hand on his shoulder} what happen!

Maanvir: {startled} DO YOU WANNA GIVE ME A HEARTATTACK.

Seeing him in such a state, everyone burst into laughing.

Maanvir: Are you all gone crazy?

Saina: leave it! Alisha so what do we now?

Alishka: Guys I think we should take the initiative

Adhiraj and Himanshu: we totally agree!

Ahaan: Not for Aleena, but Alishka and these village people am in!

Maanvir: Fine with me, what about you Saanu?

Saina: Do I have a choice? Guess not! Am in too.

Adhiraj: {excited} It means for the time being only Shadow hunters are back?

Everyone: yes

They exchanged knowing looks brimming with satisfaction, and with hands joined, they beamed with joy, as though this day had been eagerly anticipated and cherished for a lifetime.

Everyone returned back to the ashram and declared their decision to the . She smiled and asked one of her ladies to get a book. After she took them all towards a hall and in between she made them sit.

Pujaran: {smiling} I'm proud of you all, and I have full faith that you will definitely save this town.

Adhiraj: I did some research on that cave, and I found out that there's also a temple connected to it!

Pujaran: That cave is not a cursed cave, but a sacred one!

Saina: But Maa ji, how can you all imprison an evil spirit in a sacred cave?

Pujaran: The cave has two parts, one where Dravilla is present! And one where the temple is located! The part where Dravilla is present has witnessed many sacrifices, so that part is considered negative. And if you want to defeat her, you'll have to bring her to the other part of the cave!

Maanvir: Maa ji, could you please tell us how we can defeat her?

Chapter 14

Alishka: {interrupting} Before that I want you all to know something actually............
She started telling what actually happened with her.
FLASHBACK:
Alishka was sleeping peacefully in her room; A sudden thirst jolted her awake from her deep slumber. She got up and found the jug kept in her room empty, she went towards the living room and took water from the jug kept there. While drinking the water, its taste seemed alerted, and she noticed the surrounding appearing slightly blurry.

The evening light streaming through a nearby window captivated her attention, revealing a beautiful view. While mesmerized by the beauty before her, she couldn't shake the feeling that something was still amiss. Turning around, she discovered Adhiraj standing uncomfortably close, his gaze fixed on the same spot as hers.

She glanced at him, but his unwavering gaze remained fixed on the same spot, seemingly oblivious to her attempts to get his attention. Despite calling out his name, he remained unresponsive, making her feel as though she were invisible to him. After a few moments, he finally turned around, alerted by the distant sound of a door opening, leaving her in disbelief at his delayed response. It was Ahaan getting out and same conversation between them.

She observed their entire conversation, attempting to call out to them, but her efforts proved futile, intensifying the sensation of her invisibility. Suddenly noticing a nearby mirror, she approached it, only to be shocked by the absence of her reflection, adding to the surreal nature of the situation. After a few moments of bewilderment, she came to the realization that she was experiencing an out-of-body phenomenon, explaining why no one could hear or sense her presence. It was a familiar sensation, as she had experienced it since childhood, albeit never as vividly as now.

Racing towards her room to reunite with her body, she was met with a terrifying shock. She was horrified to witness her body suspended in the air, mouth gaping open in a chilling sight. She watched in alarm as a thick, black smoke rushed into her body at lightning speed, causing her suspended form to thrash and convulse uncontrollably with each passing second. In a state of panic and fear, she attempted to intervene and save her body, but it was already too late. With a sense of urgency, she dashed To Saina's room.

Before rushing away, she witnessed her lifeless body springing to life, adorned with a wicked smile and glowing red eyes, sending a shiver down her spine. She let out a wicked laugh and attempted to seize her soul, but fortunately, it managed to evade her grasp as it fled. As she sprinted through the hallway towards her room, she encountered Ahaan joyfully heading in the same direction. Desperately, she tried to halt his progress by calling out to him and blocking his path, but her efforts proved futile.

BACK TO PRESENT

Alishka: after that you guys know.

The revelation left everyone in a state of disbelief and shock, struggling to comprehend the surreal events that had unfolded.

Adhiraj: {embarrassed} Was I standing really close to you?

Ahaan: {disbelief} When she threw me into the air, you saved me?

Alishka just smiled and nodded.

Pujaran: Alishka, since when do you have this power within you?

Alishka: Yes... I... don't... myself... know... yes. Sometimes in childhood... then one day... mother... had performed a ritual... and sealed... it.

Pujaran: {sleek smile} If you all want to save us, then at least stay for two days, learn some rituals, understand about her, get trained in your language, and then go and fight!

Saina: {joining her hands} as you say Maa Ji.

Maanvir: But Mother, is there no danger from that witch here?

Pujaran: {squinting her brow} No, this is a sacred place, you are not in any danger here.

Dhriti Aka Pujaran {Devil in disguise}

Also known as Pujaran She is renowned for her wise and empathetic nature. Her skill in healing others sets her apart; she is a devout follower of God, dedicating her life to prayer and is revered as a saint. Despite being blessed with remarkable abilities, she spent her entire life grappling with hardship, seeking solace in prayer to God. Yet, the sorrow of losing her sister weighs heavily on her heart, burdening her with pain. Her nurturing demeanor endeared her to many, making her a beloved and trustworthy individual.

Or maybe all this is just a good Pretend.

Dravilla: {the main villain or villainess of our story}

Her powers are vast and terrible. She can manipulate shadows, summon storms, and twist reality itself. The cave walls echo with her mournful cries, a symphony of anguish that reverberates through time. Some say she feeds on lost souls, drawing them deeper into her web until they become mere echoes of their former selves. she's known to Dhriti's sister but is she really? is that story true?

Daaniya

"She embodies wisdom, divinity, and solidarity. Blessed with the ability of mind control, mind travel, and sensing energies, she has devoted her life to God and helping others in need. Her positive aura sets her apart. According to her, she has achieved everything in her life except love from a partner

She endured the heartache of losing her parents at a tender age yet found solace and nurturing within the walls of an ashram. There, she was enveloped by immense love and care, which became the cornerstone of her resilience and growth

Chapter 15

"Enveloped in a storm of anger, Dravilla unleashed her fury upon the brick walls, propelling herself into the air with an otherworldly force. Eyes ablaze with rage, her piercing screams echoed, sending bats into a frantic frenzy, turning the scene into a chaotic whirlwind of wrath."

Bound in heavy shackles, Aleena sat with bruises dotting her body, tears streaming down her face as she grappled with the weight of her selfishness. Lifeless hands covered her ears, attempting to drown out the echoes of her anger

Exhausted by the relentless noise, she pleaded with tearful desperation for it to cease, her voice trembling with the weight of her sorrow.

Upon hearing her plea, her anger intensified, and without mercy, she retrieved her lash, unleashing its punishing blows upon herself, consumed by a relentless fury devoid of compassion.

Aleena: {in pain} Nonoo, nooo, don't beat me, please please, why are you causing me so much pain?

Dravilla: {fuming in anger} YOUR SUFFERING GIVES ME PEACE! AND DON'T WORRY, IN A FEW DAYS YOUR SISTER WILL BE WITH YOU TOO. NOW, CALL HER!

Girl: {concentrating} Mother, Dravilla is very angry today, she's causing a lot of pain to Aleena!

Dhriti: {sternly} Hmm, this was bound to happen! Anyway, have you prepared the medicine?

Girl: {opening her eyes} Yes, but can I meet them?

Dhriti: {sleek smile} Yes, they are coming!

The door behind her opened and our experts were there. As they entered the room, they say a young woman, wearing a colorful Saree, with bright smile and beautiful hair, sitting on a holy stone and waiting for them.

Dhriti: {smiling} Daaniya! Meet our Rakshak{Saviour}

Saying this she introduced everyone to her.

Dhriti: And children, meet her, she's Daaniya, the most skilled and intelligent Pujaran of this place, just like Saina, who has the power to control your minds...

Daaniya: I not only have control over minds, but I can also use the speed of my mind to find out what's happening in other places.

Everyone: It was a pleasure to meet you.

Daaniya: {sleek smile} you all can call me Daaniya!

Saina: {smiling} Daaniya? Can you tell us what's the condition of Aleena right now?

Alishka: I know she's in pain! Her screams echo in my ears, every moment she's screaming my name, asking for help, and here I am standing helpless.

Saina: Then we should take action as soon as possible, if she's done something to Aleena...

Dhriti: {interrupting} She won't do anything to Aleena.

Everyone looked at her with disbelief

Dhriti: It's been three years, but Aleena is still alive! Alishka she is waiting for you; she wants to sacrifice both of you sisters to become free...

Alishka: {with a grave expression} But Maa Ji, can't we bear to see her suffer like that?

Daaniya: {interrupting} Mother is right, now listen to me. Two days later is the full moon night, then you can attack her, until then, prepare yourselves, bring your weapons.

Ahaan: Mother, but how can we defeat her?

Dhriti: I have a solution, but for now, today, you guys plan your strategy in your language, and come up with your plan, tomorrow I will tell you the method.

Maanvir: Mother, do you have any picture of Dravilla?

Dhriti: {narrowing her eyebrows} YES, but why?

Adhiraj: Can we plz have a look at it?

Listening to this, she nodded and clapped twice, two ladies appeared in front of them, and Dhriti instructed them to get an album

Danniya: It's time for me to Meditate! Please go outside!

Everyone did as instruct, they went out and were led into same office area, they were sitting a day before.

A lady brought a thin holy book covered in rod cloth, she handed it over to Dhriti, bowed and left the room

As she unveiled the crimson cloth, a ripple of energy swept through the entire room. Every occupant sat there, entranced by its exquisite beauty. The book, adorned in glistening gold designs, radiated a captivating allure. As she turned the pages, the ancient book revealed a tapestry of lives. Within its worn, parchment leaves, faded images captured moments of joy, sorrow, and everyday existence. Faces etched in time gazed back at her—the villagers, their stories woven into the very fabric of the land. Each photograph whispered secrets, echoes of generations, bridging the gap between past and present.

She stopped at the tenth page where there were many paintings of young women. She picked a paining of women wearing black saree, wheatish complexion.

Dhriti: {handing over} this is one and only picture, in which she is a little human

Saina: {whispering to Alishka} the real example of Don't judge a book by cover.

Maanvir: {snatching the picture} do this first. By the way Maa ji this looks like a painting.

Dhriti: {smiling} In our times, getting pictures clicked was a city thing, we were village folks, that's why we had more faith in paintings.

Adhiraj: Maa ji, did your father never forbid Dravilla from wearing black clothes?

Dhriti: {smiling} No, because he believed that no color is ever wrong.

Alishka: {pointing at a picture} Maa ji is that you?

Dhriti followed her finger and smiled at that picture, she took out the pic, stared at it for a while and finally spoke.

Dhriti: yes, that's Me, young me.

She handed that over to Aliksha, for taking a look.

Himanshu: {showing a picture in his laptop} maa Ji I guess this is her recent pic.

His words captured everyone's attention as their eyes darted toward the laptop screen, terrified by the image they saw. They encountered an image of a woman with bloodshot red eyes and long, jet-black nails, a picture that sent shivers down their spines.

Chapter 16

Dhriti: This was made by an artist named Rishabh, this is a painting from that time when the terror began to spread in Alanchal. The painter saw Dravilla wandering in his garden one day. It is said that Dravilla killed him when he made this painting.

Adhiraj: {with a grave expression} There's a big difference between these two paintings, but one thing is clear, how big a demon can hide inside a human, she's a living example of that.

Everyone simply agreed with him.

Himanshu: Wait, all our equipment is in the hotel, Adi, I think we should get them.

Ahaan: {squinting} Why did you guys bring paranormal gadgets here?

Maanvir: {adding} Did you guys know that something was wrong here?

Saina: And yes, I remember what they said when we came here. A place like ours?

Seeing the conversation getting heated up, Dhriti simply excused herself and left them alone.

Alishka: {crossing her arms} Why are you all quiet?

Adhiraj: You guys might be forgetting that even if you are not in the paranormal field now, me and Himanshu are still there

Himanshu: {adding} We like to carry our equipment's with us!

Maanvir: Just like the old days.

Lady: Mother sent these, it's her order that if you want to go outside the ashram, you should wear this.

A lady entered with a plate in her hand

Saying that she took out a roll of holy thread and tied into everyone's wrist.

Afterward, Adhiraj and Himanshu departed the location, taking a moment to inquire about necessary items from the hotel before their departure. Meanwhile, the other four individuals readied themselves for the impending confrontation. Everyone was engrossed in their preparations. Maanvir meticulously scoured the internet for any information available about the devil, while Saina delved into the historical records, piecing together a vivid image of the devil and strategies on how to combat her. Ahaan also immersed himself in ancient texts, carefully studying the provided pictures from Dhriti and amalgamating all the information to form a comprehensive understanding. Everyone else was occupied with their tasks, while Alishka remained near the window, appearing serene on the outside but battling a storm within. A war raged inside her mind and heart, causing nervousness and panic. Despite her efforts to calm herself, the desperate cries of her sister, pleading for salvation from the devil, only intensified her anxiety.

Everyone was so engulfed in their activities that they didn't realize how swiftly the time passed away.

After three hours both Adhiraj and Himanshu came back with all the stuffs, after a while everyone was called for lunch. A lady guided them towards the ashram's bustling kitchen area, resembling a vibrant bhandara, where visitors were seated and enjoying their lunch. The expansive hall was teeming with people, some serving food while others savoured their meals. After having lunch, they all went to rest a bit as the day was really exhausting.

Ahaan: Adi? Did you get my laptop?

Adhiraj: Yes sir, and everyone take your stuff and rest, in evening we will make the strategy to deal with this witch.

Everyone simply agreed with him and went to their respected chambers, Alishka was still in her trance, she was all silent and her eyes lost in infinity. She was sharing room with Ahaan.

Ahaan: Todays day was really hectic, I hope there are no work emails coming, or else dad is going to kill me.

His words broke her trance and it too few seconds to know her surroundings. Alishka was unaware that Ahaan has become the CEO of the same company he used to hate years back and she was taken aback by his statement of work email.

Alishka: {questioningly]: Work emails? On holidays?

Ahaan: {smirking}: There are no holidays for a CEO.

Alishka: {widening her eyes with shock}: A CEO?

Ahaan: {smirking} There are a lot of things darling you still don't know.

Alishka: {crossing her arms} Can't Believe you!

Suddenly, a knock on the door echoed through the room, capturing everyone's attention in an instant. Ahaan rose swiftly and swung the door open, only to be greeted by a trembling figure, drenched and terror-stricken, with a sizable gash marring his forehead. It was Himanshu who was shivering and mumbling something.

Ahaan: {terrified} Himanshu what happen? Is everything ok?

They heard the sound of footsteps approaching their room, prompting him to investigate the source. He was shoved into the room by Adhiraj, who promptly shut the door behind them both.

CHAPTER 17

"Few moments before

Saina entered her room shared with Maanvir and took a deep sigh. She stretched her arms and went towards the window to see the view. Maanvir went behind and rubbed his hand on her Sholders.

Maanvir: What happened darling?

Saina: {laying her head on his chest} Nothing just a little frustrated.

Maanvir: May I ask why?

Saina: {deep sigh} Vir I really wanted a vacation. You know how stressful it is to be a teacher!

Maanvir didn't reply he just wrapped his hand around her chest and back hugged her.

Maanvir: well, everyone's tired and resting right now, so do you want to go for a trek?

Saina: {with a bright smile} Yeah sure but where?

Maanvir: Well, I have heard about a beautiful water fall nearby.

Saina: {jumping with excitement} What are we waiting for let's go!

Maanvir saw her with a beautiful smile. They both left their rooms without informing anyone, being it an old habit. Upon reaching the same flower field, Saina held Maanvir's hands tightly and started running like a small child.

Maanvir: aree saina aram se mein gir jaunga. {Siana be careful or else I will fall down}

Saina: {catching her breath} Main tumhe kabhi nahi girne dungi {I will never let you fall down}

After a good run of half a kilometer they could see a stunning waterfall cascades gracefully from the heights of the hills, embraced by lush greenery, where the crystal-clear water dances with the wind, creating a mesmerizing symphony of sound.

Saina: {keeping her hand on her chest} It's so beautiful, Alanchal is really a beautiful place, I feel bad for the people living here.

Maanvir: {smiling} Come on Saina let's go down.

Maanvir took her hand in his and they went down, the path was little steep with green grass and trees. But the view was mesmerizing. It took 45 minutes for them reach down near the waterfall.

Maanvir: {smiling} Finally, we made it!

They spotted a beautiful rock nearby and decided to sit on it.

Saina: {with mischievous smile} Viru! I want to go in.

Maanvir: {smirking} Ok as you say soon to be Mrs. Singh.

Saina was a little confused and surprised to hear this Before she could comprehend anything, he swept her into his arms and leaped into the waterfall's embrace.

Saina: {shouting} THE WATER IS SO COLD.

Hearing her reaction, he swiftly carried her out of the waterfall's embrace and helped her stand on solid ground. Drenched from head to toe, water droplets cascading from every direction, it took her a moment to clear her eyes and blink them wide open. As she opened her eyes, she playfully punched him on his hips, eliciting a slight groan of mock pain from him. He chuckled softly, then gently pulled her closer by her waist, while she wrapped her arms around his neck, maintaining a slight gap between them.

Maanvir: {panting} feeling like vacation now?

Saina: {panting} of course and happy too.

Dravilla: Oh, really but not for long.

Upon hearing the demonic voice, they swiftly parted from each other, scanning their surroundings anxiously to locate the source, a shiver of fear coursing through their spines.

Dravilla: look up!

As the voice echoed once more, they instinctively gazed upward towards the azure sky, only to behold her ominous figure soaring amidst a swirl of black smoke and bats. Adorned in a black saree, her eyes glowed crimson, and her chilling smile sent shivers down their spines.

Saina: What do you want? Why are you here?

Dravilla: {smiling evilly} Didn't my dear sister talk already about me Saina?

Himanshu: Saina, Maanvir waha se zaldi hatoo. {Saina, Maanvir get away from there Now!}

As Dravilla heard his voice, she turned and as she did Adhiraj threw a pile of dust on her which was a holy sand given to them by Dhriti, but unfortunately it missed, making her angry.

Dravilla: {laughing} YOU MADE A HUGE MISTAKE.

Uttering those words, two additional hands materialized on her back, expanding in size and seizing them both with an unyielding grip.

Saina: {crying} Leave us alone, nooo, Maanvirrrr

Maanvir: Himanshu get help before it's too late...

She sprayed a black smoke onto their faces making them unconscious, she turned around to capture Himanshu and Adhiraj but in the nick of time both ran away and hide themselves. They were hiding near the waterfall behind a big rock, they saw her taking Saina and Maanvir inside the waterfall and disappeared. After hiding for 5 mins, they came out and were fear stricken and panting.

Adhiraj: {angrily} SHIT! What do we now?

Himanshu: {angrily} ITS JUST BECAUSE YOU MISSED!

Adhiraj: {angrily} OH, COME ON AS IF YOURE BULLS EYE.

Himanshu was already frustrated and angry and hearing his words made him lose his temper, he punched him real hard on his stomach making his growl in pain, Adhiraj held him through his collar and pushed to the ground. Suddenly it started raining and they started hearing evil laugh of dravilla and screams off Saina and Maanvir. They both ran towards the Ashram towards the Ahaan and Alishka and gave this terrifying news.

Ahaan: {slamming his hand on the wall} ARE YOU SERIOUS? ADI HOW COULD YOU MISS IT? AND WHY DID SAINA AND MAANVIR WENT ALONE THAT TOO FAR AWAY FROM AASHRAM? WERE THEY NOT WEARING THEIR OM?

Alishka: Ahaan, it's not time to fight, it's time to save, guys let's do this now only we got no time, I can hear Saina calling for help, we should go right now!

Ahaan: But wait a sec! how did you know there were in danger?

Adhiraj: I was working on my equipment's when Daaniya came running towards our room and informed us that our friend's lives is in danger.

Alishka: she is quite a beauty.

Himanshu: {panting} Yes but before that lets get ready and save our friends.

Adhiraj: Guys come near, okexecuting our mission no 99 Alishka and Ahaan you guys will first enter thecave from the hotel side I and Himanshu from the waterfall, Alishka and Ahaantake walkie talkie and night vision cameras with you. we all will be connected through walkie talkie and please come back alive. let's go.

EVERYONE: YES SIR

CHAPTER 18

Everyone got ready immediately taking the necessary measures, before leaving their home Ahaan and Alishka shared a brief eye contact and left for Adhiraj and Himanshu's room. Himanshu was still angry with Adhiraj on missing the dust just because of his clumsiness. He wasn't replying any of his words simply getting ready for a war ahead.

Adhiraj: {slightly irritated} Himanshu! I am sorry, why are you ignoring me like that, I didn't do this on purpose.

Himanshu: YOU HAVE ANY IDEA? WHAT PAIN DRAVILLA MIGHT BE GIVING TO SIANA AND MAANVIR? AND YOURE SAYING SORRY? SORRY DOSENT MAKE A DEAD PERSON ALIVE.

Adhiraj: {angered} SO WHAT SHOULD I DO NOW? I AM TELLING YOU PLZ STOP THIS ATTITUDE OF YOURS.

Himanshu: {crossing his hands} OR WHAT? HUH?

Adhiraj shot him a death glare. But he didn't do anything. Simply turned around to see for the objects.

Himanshu: {smirking} Yes exactly, turning your back and doing nothing.

Those words ignited his temper, prompting him to rise abruptly, pivot towards Himanshu, and seize him by the collar, forcefully pushing him to the ground. As Himanshu fell to the ground, he swiftly sprang back up, launching himself into a powerful punch aimed at his adversary's chest. Engulfed by frustration and anger, they engaged in a fierce brawl, each blow unleashing pent-up emotions as they grappled with each other in the throes of combat. On the other hand, as Alishka and Ahaan came near their room, Amidst the cacophony of crashing objects and the sounds of their struggle, they both agreed to burst into the room, only to discover them lying on the floor, locked in a fierce combat stance.

Alishka: {shocked} Adi, Himanshu what's going on? Why are you fighting like kids?

They both got separated and Ahaan helped them to stand up.

Ahaan: {glaring} Their lives are in danger there and you people are fighting here?

Adhiraj: I am Sorry, I just got angry.

Himanshu: I am sorry too.

Alishka: {smiling} Ok then let's save our friends.

Everyone agreed with her, Adhiraj handed over the night vision cameras, and walkie talkies to Alishka and Ahaan.

After they all straight head to office area where they all sat earlier. Dhriti was waiting for them, as they entered the room, they saw almost all the lady staff who worked there was present there. Everyone was looking with a lost hope in their eyes towards them.

Daaniya: You guys are going to do a big job; may God give you strength and you succeed.

Himanshu: {sigh}We will emerge only after success.

Dhriti: First come to the temple with us, take blessings of God.

Following the instructions, they proceeded to the temple along with everyone else. Upon arrival, they respectfully removed their shoes and cleansed their hands with water before entering the sacred space. Upon entering the temple, they were greeted by its vastness, adorned with images of various gods and goddesses adorning the walls. As they ventured deeper, they encountered a magnificent and sizable idol of Lord Shiva, Maha Parvati, and Lord Ganesh, seated majestically in their divine presence. The priest, present in the temple, warmly greeted them and applied a tilak on their foreheads as a blessing. He then took marigold flowers and sprinkled holy water over them, invoking blessings for their well-being.

Daaniya: Pandit ji, please do a small puja. These are our protectors.

Pandit ji reverently brought out the aarti thali and began preparing for the puja. He lit the Diya with camphor and agarbattis, filling the air with the soothing fragrance of roses, calming their minds and spirits as they immersed themselves in the divine atmosphere of the ceremony. After performing the aarti with devotion, Pandit ji offered the aarti to all the members present, allowing each one to receive the divine blessings and grace of the ceremony.

Panditji: {warm smile} By the grace of Mata Rani, you all return healthy and safe.

All of them touched his feet and promised everyone to return safely, but before going Daaniya took Aliksha to a secluded spot to talk.

Daaniya: Alishka we don't have much time to explain everything, but listen to this very carefully, you need to do these three things to save your sister and defeat dravilla, I will be connected with you through your mind. Now firstly try to bring her to part of the cave Dhriti Maa told you, I and she will be present there, secondly you will find 6 knives in the temple give three to Ahaan and keep three with you remember give them only to Ahaan, moreover you and Ahaan have to stab those knives on her back that together that's the way you will be able to defeat her and third and most important thing, Dravilla will try to play with your emotions and minds don't be a fool to get played . all the best Alishka.

Alishka: Daaniya just one question how will I find the knives?

Daaniya: I will guide you through mind.

After that she joined her head with Alishka forming a connection between.

Alishka's eyes sparkled with determination as she joined the trio. As they exited the ashram, a palpable sense of confusion, fear, and tension lingered in their minds, yet none uttered a word, each grappling with their thoughts in silence. After walking for a mile, they naturally split into two pairs, each forming a duo as they continued their journey ahead.

Adhiraj: {taking a sigh} Ok Ahaan and Alishka, all the best, I hope we meet soon.

Ahaan just nodded his head with grave expression and parted ways.

The journey unfolded with Ahaan and Alishka walking together, while Adhiraj and Himanshu formed the other pair. Despite the challenges looming ahead, the unresolved tension between Adhiraj and Himanshu persisted, casting a shadow over their path. Despite being together, Ahaan and Alishka found their minds troubled by numerous unanswered questions about each other, casting a veil of uncertainty over their bond.

The outcome remains uncertain; whether they will successfully rescue their friends or fall into Dravilla's trap, granting her the opportunity to escape the cave and seize dominion over the world, is yet to be revealed.

Chapter 19

Both pairs were standing into the entrance of cave, they could hear the evil laughs of dravilla echoing. Alishka controlled her mind, as the screams of her Aleena sister were getting louder and louder causing her to get in a panic stage, she was taking long deep breaths to maintain her mind composure. Ahaan who was all set for the mission took a deep breath, he casually glanced at Alishka and discovering her in this vulnerable state, he reached out and gently took her hand. As she felt his touch, she shared a fleeting yet meaningful eye contact with him.

Ahaan: {reassuring} Alishu! We will make it out alive!

Alishka: {shaking her head} Yes!

After that brief interaction they took out night vision cameras and stuck them in their collars, took out headlight and all the equipment and were all set to enter the cave. They both shared eye contact again.

Together: Let's do this!

They ventured into the unknown, into a realm akin to hell, bracing themselves for challenges unforeseen.

On the other hand, Adhiraj and Himanshu wore caps and night vision googles, they tightened their backpacks and were all set for the rescue. They just looked at each other and nodded. After that they kept their feet in the ice-cold water and ventured towards the waterfall, they saw a black hole behind the milk white water fall and as they stepped forward, the om bracelet around their wrists began to tighten, causing excruciating pain as if squeezing their fists relentlessly.

Himanshu: Maa ji warned us about it

Adhiraj: Cover it with your coat sleeve.

Over here as Aliksha and Ahaan were going deeper and deeper, the screams were becoming louder and louder in Alishka's mind. They were giving her a big headache; she would have lost her mind if Ahaan wasn't there by her side holding her arm and leading the way. Ahaan being deeply immersed in knowing the surrounding and leading the way being unaware about her situation. Suddenly they both heard a loud cry, from behind. They both swinged around to search what it was but found nothing.

Ahaan: I guess we need to be more careful, as all her traps have started working.

Alishka just weakly nodded, they continued their journey until they reached the place where they saw beautiful stones shinning in the dark everywhere, but the problem here was that tunnel was distributed here into two rows.

Ahaan: {deep breath} Alishka, I guess we need to part ways, each choosing a path to follow.

Alishka: {broken voice} Ahaan I can't do this alone.

Upon hearing her words, he turned towards her with a mixture of shock and disbelief written across his face. As he glanced at her, he noticed tears welling up in her eyes, her face drained of color and trembling with fear. According to him, a woman who was once fearless, joyful, and deeply passionate about her work, now appeared terrified, shattered, and haunted by fear. She gazed at him with teary eyes, her expression filled with a mixture of sadness and longing. Suddenly, she found herself once again engulfed by the chilling echoes of her sister's desperate pleas for freedom. She began experiencing panic attacks, causing her body to shake and shiver uncontrollably in fear. She teetered on the brink of falling, but he swiftly reached out and caught her by the waist, preventing her from crashing and hitting her head on the unforgiving stone below.

Ahaan: {astounded} Alishka calm down, control your breaths, plz we need you, I need you. Calm down, take some deep breaths.

Alishka although being in a state of panic still somehow was able to hear him and did as instruct after a matter of 10 mins, she was completely normal. As she returned to her normal state, he enveloped her in a tight hug, his own fear evident in his desperate need to comfort her after witnessing her distress. She clung to him, her sobs echoing the turmoil raging within her as the weight of recent events threatened to shatter her from the inside out.

Daaniya: Alishka I know what you're going through, your sister voices or her plea are making you go insane, but from now on they won't disturb as I am connected with you.

Listening to her voice a brought a sense of peace, she closed her eyes for a min. Ahaan reluctantly broke the hug and he cupped her face.

Ahaan: Look Alishu, I know it's hard for you, but now it's not only the matter of your sister's life but our friends too. We need to stay strong and complete this mission.

Alishka: {opening her eyes} I understand. {taking a deep breath} stay connected with me through walkie talkies. And I want you back alive.

Ahaan: {chuckling} Yes, my dear, after this we have to talk a lot.

. After making their choices and exchanging glances, they each stepped onto their respective paths, disappearing into the unknown.

On the other hand, as Adhiraj and Himanshu were entering deeper and deeper, and a rotten smell and black smoke was giving them a headache and raising their anger. As they dig deeper and deeper they it was getting darker. Himanshu saw something and grabbed Adhiraj by his collar and hid behind a rock.

Himanshu: {whispering} Adhiraj? Look over there.

Adhiraj just followed his figure and was shocked, they both looked towards each other is tension, as if what to do next? They saw Dravilla floating in air, with her jet-black hair floating in air and her eyes as red-hot ember, open wide and black smoke flowing near her.

Adhiraj: {extremely low tone} what do we do now?

Himanshu patted on his shoulder and pointed towards something or someone. As he followed his fingers, he saw Aleena lying like a dead corpse in a corner with shackles all over hands and legs.

Himanshu: Where are our friends?

Adhiraj: I can't see them either.

Himanshu: [shocked} That's Maa ji!

He followed his eyes to witness an unbelievable sight, leaving him in a state of utter dilemma, torn between disbelief and uncertainty.

They both watched in astonishment as Dhriti entered the cave, carrying a torch, observing her enter the cave, she descended from the air and stood firmly on her feet. At first, their eyes met with a sharp glare, but soon that glare transformed into a wicked smile. They approached each other and embraced, their reunion marked by a mixture of mischief and camaraderie. As they released from the embrace, Dhriti underwent a startling transformation. Her form morphed from that of a normal woman in ordinary attire to that of an evil witch, her eyes ablaze with a fiery red hue, a wicked smile curling upon her lips. Her hair cascaded around her, untamed and flowing in the air, emphasizing the aura of malevolence that surrounded her.

Dhriti: {wicked smile} "And sister, how are you? Did you like the gift?"

Dravilla: {groaning} "Yes sister, I am fine. But playing with this gift is not fun. Bring more gifts."

Dhriti: {evil chuckle} oh my dear little sister didn't I send two gifts in the morning and now four of them?

Dravilla: "Oh yes Didi, but now I want to play Chakrayudh."

Dhriti: ok as you wish my little one, cause all of them are nearby.

Listening to this both of them were in utter shock, they looked at each other with shock but before they could turn back their faces were swiftly shrouded in a thick black cloth, while an ominous black smoke billowed around them, suffocating their senses. In the blink of an eye, they succumbed to the overpowering darkness, slipping into unconsciousness. All the holy things worn by them were thrown away at a blink of eye. Their unconscious bodies floated including Maanvir and Saina eerily in the air, suspended by an unseen force amidst the swirling darkness. Dhriti and dravilla laughed evilly looking at them.

On the other hand, Alishka navigated through a narrow tunnel illuminated by shimmering pebbles scattered along the path. Each pebble glinted with a deceptive allure, their edges razor-sharp, threatening to cut through anything that dared to touch them. He too ventured through the narrow tunnel; its path illuminated by glimmering pebbles casting a deceptive light. Emerging simultaneously from the other end, they reunited, their paths converging once more in an unexpected twist of fate. As their eyes met once again a relief of peace swirled through their but this contact was broken by the crazy laughter sound.

Daaniya: This laugh? Alishka, can you go a little bit further.

Alishka did as request and signaled Ahaan to follow her. As they entered the source of the laughter, they were equally stunned to find her standing there, her presence in that place defying all logic and expectation.

Daaniya: {equally shocked} Maa ji? What is she doing here?

Before they could even contemplate hiding or fleeing, she had already become aware of their presence, leaving them with nowhere to go but to face her.

Dhriti: {evil smile} "Come, Alishka, come. I was waiting for you. Now, you are the main character of our game."

Alishka: {shocked} Maa ji? A betrayal from your side wasn't expected. How could you deceive us?

Ahaan: {gritting his teeth} I knew something was up with this lady, when she showed us the pictures, in old days wearing black wasn't allowed, how did we fall for it?

Dravilla: that's enough of time being wasted in talking, Now THE GAME WILL BEGIN

With a sinister grin, she uttered those words and then clapped twice. Instantly, a dense black smoke billowed around them, carrying a foul odor that assaulted their senses. The noxious fumes engulfed them, causing both to feel drowsy and disoriented, their consciousness slipping away. Ahaan attempted to move, but a strange numbness gripped his limbs, rendering them unresponsive. Though his mind raced with urgency, his body remained immobile, as if held in place by an invisible force. Helplessly, he watched as she succumbed to unconsciousness, a surge of panic coursing through him as he longed to reach her side, yet unable to do so.

Alishka, witnessing Ahaan's collapse, felt a surge of desperation to be by his side, yet a heavy sense of helplessness washed over her as she too struggled against the immobilizing effects of the dark magic. Despite her frantic attempts to move towards him, time seemed to slip away, leaving her standing frozen and powerless, unable to reach him in time. Suddenly, both of their bodies began to levitate in the air, suspended upright as if held by an unseen force. His body was joined by other members, yet she remained suspended in the air, isolated and vulnerable. Ahaan indulged completely into unconscious. Dravilla and Dhriti came towards Alishka, as she watched them in despair and half consciousness. Dravilla tightly cupped her face with her fingers, a gesture of frustration and agitation amidst the chaos surrounding her.

Dravilla: As you can see all your friends, stranded here. And in order to save them, you need to play a game. A GAME OF MIND MAZE.

Alishka: {with a lot of efforts} I promise you, once the games over, I am coming for you and you're going to regret it.

Dhriti: {evil chuckle} I think someone's overconfident!

She clapped her hands once again, invoking the dark magic. In response, a swirling black smoke materialized, forming smoky hands that snatched her through her curls, dragging her forcefully into a realm shrouded in impenetrable darkness. The moment she was dropped into that realm, exhaustion washed over her, lulling her into a deep slumber despite the unsettling circumstances. After four hours of profound sleep, Alishka was abruptly awakened by the jarring sounds of drums echoing loudly, causing discomfort to her ears. She gazed up to see the witch floating just five feet above her, a sinister presence casting a shadow over the dimly lit surroundings. As she opened her eyes, a sense of dread crept over her, realizing the perilous situation she was in.

Chapter 20

She emerged, looming over her with a grave expression etched upon her features. With a chilling intensity, she uttered, "Let the game begin," signalling the start of a sinister contest.

Saying she snapped her fingers and an unknown force made Alishka stand upright. Dravilla flashed into dark smoke. Being exhausted mentally, Aliksha was in a vulnerable state. Now alone, the burden of rescuing her friends rested solely on her shoulders in the midst of darkness. Now left to navigate the darkness without her steadfast companion, who had always been her rock, she felt a profound sense of weakness and despair consume her. She might have given up if Daaniya wasn't still there for her.

Daaniya: Alishka! Don't think you're Alone in this! I am with you, now we will solve this together, but if you don't want to lose me don't reply to me, just listen to me carefully.

Suddenly she heard Dravilla, she couldn't see her but a black smoke evolved over her head.

Dravilla: OK MISS OVER-CONFIDENT! YOUR FIRST STAGE OF THE GAME BEGIN. IF YOU GUESS THE RIGHT ANSWER OF THE RIDDLE, YOU ARE ONE STEP CLOSER, AND YES THAT ANSWER WILL LEAD YOU TO THE PERSON, RIGHT ANSWER TO THE PERSON, WRONG ANSWER MAY END BAD FOR THE PERSON

Alishka: {taking a deep breath} Am ready!

Daaniya: Mee too

Dravilla: RIDDLE NUMBER ONE:

I speak without a mouth and hear without ears. I have no body, but I come alive with the wind. What am I?

Alishka's eyes sparkled as she heard this riddle it was the same riddle, which was asked by Saina in college days, she used to ask it in every game of riddles.

Alishka: The answer is an echo. Echoes are sounds that bounce off surfaces and return to the listener's ears, even though they don't have a physical form.

Dravilla: {outraged} LUCK THIS TIME NOT EVERYTIME.

After that, a brilliant light pierced through the darkness, illuminating a maze adorned in vibrant shades of green.

Dravilla: YOUR FRIEND IS IN THE END OF THE MAZE! GO FIND HER IN 30 MINUTES IF YOU CAN OR ELSE......

Alishka: OR ELSE WHAAT?

She didn't hear anything further, only the echo of wicked laughter.

Daaniya: Alishka be calm, we have 30 minutes let's do it! As she said the answer will lead to the person, echo will lead to the person, follow the echo.

AS Alishka stepped inside the maze it was a quiet dead silence, there was not sound at all.

Alishka: {narrowing her eyebrows} why is there no sound or an echo? Wait a minute.... maybe this works.... {shouting} AHAAN

It brought shock at her face, as she couldn't hear her own voice, while saying his name.

Alishka: {to herself} what does this mean? I need to try one more time. {shouting} SAINA............

To her surprise this time she could her voice completely and it echoed toward a direction. She called her name numerous times and followed the echo, after reaching towards a point. That echo started to getter louder and louder as she ventured in.

Daaniya: You're doing great Alishka.

As she ventured further, Alishka's gaze fell upon a stunning red flower nestled in the midst of the maze. Its beauty was so captivating that she found herself entranced, her eyes unable to look away as if under a spell. Her mesmerized gaze lingered on the hypnotic flower, wasting precious time as its enchanting beauty threatened to ensnare her mind.

Daaniya: {shouting} ALISHKA!!!! WAKE UP!!

Alishka woke from that daydreaming and covered her eyes with her hands in order to no to fall under its spell again. As she ventured and finally reached towards the exit, she heard her name in the style Saina used to call.

Saina: {sweet melody} Alishkaaaaaa....... Cmon babe.... we will be late for school.

That was already enough for her to understand she had finally found her. After completing the maze, Alishka searched frantically for Saina and spotted her lying on the ground. With a surge of concern, she rushed towards her side.

Alishka: {patting} Siana wake up! Wake up please.

Saina: {mumbling} Alishka......save Maanvir......plz...

She hugged her tightly.

Alishka: I will save everyone.

Suddenly, Saina's body began to float into the air, ascending higher and higher until she disappeared from sight.

Dravilla: This time you were lucky next time you won't be!

Alishka: dravilla I hope you are not breaking the rules!

She submerged into thin air without giving any response. Alishka slammed her forehead with her hand.

Danniya: Alishka, relax Saina is safe. But right now, we need to know why Dhriti betrayed us.

Danniya: Look Alishka you have to complete the game by yourself, because I need to search over here and make sure everyone's Safe from that backstabber. Stay safe dear, they need you!

Listening to this Alishka felt a little shiver of fear and her eyes got moist but she somehow gathered herself and started observing her surrounding, the whole area was a serene of darkness with red crystals shinning with dim light. She turned around and found the Maze disappearing in thin air. After its disappearance the whole place turned out to be a large hall inside a mountain, with red crystal shining everywhere.

Chapter 21

After about an hour, she once more witnessed the return of a white light accompanied by the rhythmic beat of drum.

Same smoke Appeared over her heard and once again Alishka heard her sinister laugh.

Dravilla: {Sinister Grin} WELL, MISS LUCKY, OR THIS TIME NOT! I DON'T CARE! HERES YOUR SECOND RIDDLE AND AM DAMM SURE YOU WILL NOT MAKE IT!

Alishka just rolled her eyes and strengthened her arms, being set for the unknown quiz.

Dravilla: Your second quiz is here!

"I'm a twin without flesh or bone, in my world, reflections are prone. Seek your face, you'll see your own, but I'm more than just a clone. What am I?"

Alishka: {utter confusion} What? A twin without......

Dravilla: Miss overconfident. You only have 5 mins to solve, only one guess and wrong answer......

Alishka: I know! Just let me think! Flesh or bone? Refle ct......wait a minute....... I'm more than clone......

Alishka: {thinking} It must be the answer......Yes, it is....

Dravilla: Ticktock, the clocks ticking's. Oops Looks like you're losing a life.

Alishka: MIRROR.......... ITS MIRROR.

As she heard those words, she said nothing, and the smoke disappeared above Alishka's head. Shortly thereafter, a new type of maze began to take shape. It shimmered in the white room and appeared to have narrower passages compared to traditional mazes. Seeing that image, she hesitated, unsure whether to step in or not. Her uncertainty dissipated when she noticed a temporary timer materialize above her head, composed of black smoke, ticking away 30 minutes. With a deep breath, she stepped in. As she ventured forward, she discovered that the maze was constructed entirely of mirrors, each reflecting a different image of herself. Every mirror revealed a different aspect of her life, reflecting various moments and facets of her existence. As she ventured further into the maze, she encountered a reflection of herself as a child. She saw a beautiful, childish and innocent smile forming in her lips. But it didn't last even a minute.

"I HATE YOU"

Alishka turned around to see who it was and was shocked to see Aleena Glaring at her from the other side of mirror, her hand bound in chain Seeing, she became furious and punched the glass wall between them.

Alishka: Aleena? You're still hating on me.........

Aleena: {Punching the wall again} Why shouldn't I?

Alishka just ignored her words and ventured in; she was eventually led inside a circular room filled it mirror. But this time she could see Aleena's Reflections everywhere.

Dravilla: Now you have only 10 mins to think and break the glass or mirror which truly contains Aleena not her reflection and yes you have only one chance to break glass if it's wrong, she dies, GOOD Luck

Alishka was panting heavily, she turned around to observe each and every mirror. She was panting heavily, as it was all consuming her mind and making her vulnerable, unsure of what to do next. She meticulously observed every mirror surrounding her. She saw Aleena's reflection, containing an expression of anger and envy, which grew more intense the longer she looked. But one mirror caught her attention as she saw a tear running down her cheeks. She half-closed her eyes and looked closely, just to find her reflection trying hard to conceal its tears. Now she knew which mirror she had to break. She ran towards that mirror and began relentlessly pounding it with her fist. Suddenly, a baseball appeared beside her. She grabbed it and began smashing the mirror with force. The mirror shattered into pieces, finally breaking apart completely.

As Aleena saw Aliksha, tears welled in her eyes. She dropped to her knees, clasped her hands together, and began begging for forgiveness. She ran towards her and hugged her tightly, as she hadn't seen her in four long years. But before they converse Aleena's body levitating in air and she disappeared in thin air. Suddenly same black smoke surrounded Alishka and made her drift into a long sleep.

On the other side, Saina woke up near the entrance of the cave, she sat up straight taking support of a huge rock kept nearby, she was holding her head unable to process anything suddenly she saw Aleena levitating in air and was dropped to the ground at the same spot. Seeing her Saina somehow got on her feet and ran toward Aleena.

Saina: {patting her cheeks} Aleena? Wake up, wake up!

As she took her hand to check for a pulse, she was shocked to see bruise marks on her wrist. As she examined her body all over, she was even more terrified to see her vulnerable condition, with bruises present all over and certain cuts marring her skin.

Aleena: {weak voice} Am I free?

Saina: Yes, you're free, open your eyes to see the sky above.

Aleena opened her eyes slowly and tears started dwelling in her eyes as she felt the presence of fresh air with voice of water and the light of sky. A small stroke cold wind made her believe she was finally out of that hell she's been suffering in for four years.

Saina helped her to standup right. Looks like she even forgot how to walk in these four years.

Saina: I think you should wash yourself in a river nearby. You will feel better, till then I will try to contact Daaniya to get you help.

Aleena just nodded and dragged herself towards the river and splashed the fresh water all over her face

Chapter 22

Daaniya quickly uncovered her eyes as soon as her connection broke and got up in fear. She sprang to her feet, calling out everyone's names and commanding the closure of the main gates, urging them to flee toward the temple.

Daaniya: EVERYONE WHERE IS DHRITI?

Lady: Maa j.........

Daaniya: DON'T CALL THAT WITCH THAT!

Dhriti: DAANIYA, control your language, or else I will chop your tongue off.

She spun around and fixed her glare on her the moment she heard a word.

Daaniya: Guards! Capture her, she is evil

Upon hearing her order, guards rushed towards Dhriti but halted in front of her. She dashed toward them to investigate the reason for their pause, only to be stunned by the sight of her eyes glowing. Her eyes shimmered with an ethereal glow as she began to levitate in the air, casting a hypnotic spell over all the guards.

Dhriti: {sinister smile} CMON NOW, STOP STARING AT MY FACE CAPTURE HER.

Daaniya: {panicking} NO! No, no, No. Guards...... {showing them Om} Don't you dare, come near me.

Dhriti: Smart move, but it's not going to help little one.

Daaniya just winked at her and closed her eye, moving her lips, chanting a prayer. Her body started levitating in air and a light started glowing behind. Everyone present there were either stunned or confused to see what's happening. She opened her eyes, and a vibrant light escaped from them, causing everyone present to flinch and close their eyes due to its high intensity. Everyone was shocked to see her in this form.

Daaniya: {glaring}"You can control these people, but not me. I've had this power inside me for a long time, and I didn't let you know because I doubted you, but that doubt has turned into confidence today."

Dhriti: {smirking}"Actually, I don't need you. I'll succeed in my goals even without you. But it's necessary to remove you from the path. However, no matter, you go ahead and help them. But when we defeat them and make them our slaves, what will I do with you, you can't even imagine."

Before Dhriti could talk more Daaniya disappeared in thin air.

Dhriti seized control in ashram and hypnotized everyone. She closed the gates of the main temple luckily the Pandit was sleeping in his chamber inside the temple, so Dhriti couldn't threaten him. She removed every holy thing in the temple which could come in her path. After that she unsealed a secret door present in Ashram, the same door she used to visit Dravilla. She led everyone inside the tunnel and entered a large room, Covered with red crystals all over. A huge fire was lit up at the center of the room. Dhriti clapped thrice and as soon as she did that, a black cloud appeared and formed into the shape of a woman, none other than Dravilla, her eyes red covered in black liquid and her face slowly turning into a skull and her hairs flowing. She was standing there as a robot.

Slowly everyone presents there came back to their senses. They all were in a state of panic.

Over here Adhiraj, Himanshu, Ahaan and Maanvir were lying unconscious. Adhiraj was coming back to consciousness slowly. He unleashed his eyes and found himself sitting in a familiar boat.

"Adhiraj?" a girl called for him.

Hearing those words, he turned around and found a girl staring at him with a comfort smile.

Adhiraj: Udita? Omg where am I?

Udita: Don't you remember this place; it was our favorite place.

Adhiraj: {smiling} Yes Udita, I remember it with all my heart, and I really miss you really do.

Udita: you didn't move on even after 10 years....

Adhiraj: 10 years, 8 months, 2 weeks, 3 days.

Udita: {smiling} Raj, I wish I could talk more but now you need to wake up.

Adhiraj: {squinting} Why? I need you.

Udita: WAKE UP! NOW

'ADHITRAJJJJJJJJJJJJJ'

Listen to his name he popped his head up and saw Himanshu screaming his name and telling him to wake up. As he popped down, he saw a terrifying figure.

Udita: {in a terrible state} I SAID WAKE UPP!

Hearing that terrible voice and encountering that breathtaking shape of hers, Adhiraj woke up gasping for each breath.

Himanshu: {breathing heavily} Maanvir, Adi is also awake.

Maanvir: Oh great, Ahaan is also opening his eyes.

It took a minute's time for Adhiraj and Ahaan to wake up properly and observe the surroundings. They found themselves in a dark side of the cave with red crystals glowing everywhere and a glass type of wall towards their left

Ahaan: {smirking} We all are caught in a really big mess, this time.

Maanvir: {Panting} Truly, but how did we get here, or I should ask now how do we get out of here and where are the girls? Himanshu: {squeezing his eyes at a distant figurine} Who's that levitating in air.

Adhiraj: {joining in} Alishka? Is that her?

Listening to her name, Maanvir and Ahaan both got up and ran towards the wall. Ahaan recognized her in one go.

Ahaan: {slamming his hand on the wall} That Alisha, is she asleep....and wait it's not glass but thick ice.

Maanvir: If Alisha's here! Where's Saina?

Ahaan: {gritting his teeth} we need to find a way to get out of.........

He was interrupted by the sudden appearance of black clouds above them. Those clouds took the formation of Dravilla.

Dravilla : {sinister grin} Wow all the pretty handsome man are awake. And what were you saying Ahaan, find a way to get out of here? Well, you people don't have to take any pain on that, but your friend does.

Adhiraj: What do you mean?

Dravilla didn't bother to reply instead she clapped her hands twice making all four them to levitate in the air.

Maanvir: Where are you taking us? Where's Saina?

As he said this, he was dropped in a glass container. The glass container being half of his height making him uncomfortable and his body in pain.

After that Himanshu was dropped a maze made of bush. As he landed on a green grass, his hands were tied with the roots of trees and a knife formed farther from him.

After that Adhiraj was dropped into a pool of water. the water was extremely hot, but the temperature of water was dropping every minutes.

And finally, Ahaan was dropped in a dark Alley. He wasn't able to spot a single thing and due to darkness, he also dropped his glasses somewhere making his vision blurry.

Dravilla: {sinister Grin} I hope Alishka is not able to find you all. Don't worry she won't be able to.

With another double clap of her hands, a figure levitated in the air and was then dropped to the ground. It was Alishka, she rose to her feet, her eyes ablaze with anger and hatred as she looked at her.

Alishka: YOU WILL REGERT EACH AND EVERY ACTION OF YOURS.

CHAPTER 23

Dravilla: First solve this.

I'm made of sand, yet crystal clear. I hold your drink or something dear. I come in different shapes and sizes, From fragile flutes to jars for spices. What am I?

Alishka: {smirking} A GLASS CONTAINER.........

Dravilla: {shocked} I like you for a reason.

As she uttered those words. A light illuminated a medium-sized square container, revealing Maanvir in a vulnerable condition.

Alishka: {shocked} MAANVIR!

Dravilla: {sinister grin} you have 10 minutes to save him and one more thing the glass container will shrink ever minute so good luck.

Alishka ran towards container and started pounding in the glass, but it was of no use. Maanvir gestured her towards an end. She followed his fingers and found a code lock. She was confused to see number in it. She did the

360 of the containers looked up and down to find any clue unaware that 2 mins have already passed, and the container has shrunk twice making it extremely uncomfortable for Maanvir to sit inside. Suddenly something clicked her mind, and she held the lock in her hands and began entering specific digits. And to her surprise the code was correct it removed the glass and Maanvir was all free. Alishka helped him to get back on his feet although his body aching due to the uncomfortable posture, he was in for the past 5 minutes.

Maanvir: OH MY GOD! That's the worst case I have been through.

Alishka: Thank God that code was correct. But I don't understand!

Maanvir: Leaving everything, just tell me is Saina, ok?

Alishka: {soft smile} Yes, she's fine. In fact, you are also supposing to teleport to her but......

Maanvir: Meaning?

Alishka explained him all about the game they all are stuck in.

Maanvir: Well, maybe she has another plan.

Dravilla: {from afar} Correct Guessing. Now you two have to choose a maze to rescue your loved team members.

CHALLENGE 2: TWO MAZE

As she spoke those words a shiny light emerged opening two doorways. One door made of simple wet wood, and another made of wood with a grass coating all over it.

Alishka: {pointing} I will choose the grass one.

Maanvir: {crossing his hands} Hmm ok. Let's solve this maze.

They exchanged brief looks and approached the door. Before entering, they gave each other a thumbs-up and conveyed a message to stay safe through their eyes.

Alishka: {in mind} Plz Ahaan I want to find you this time.

Being unaware that her mind was somehow connected to Ahaan and listening to her voice after a long time Ahaan felt relieved.

Maanvir entered and saw a maze filled with water.

Maanvir: It means I need to swim again.

He jumped in the water that was a little hot. Sensing the high temperature his whole body turned red. But the temperature was dropping every minute.

Maanvir: Oh god, wait a minute the temperature's dropping I need to find the person fast.

He swam along the stream, trying his best to find any clues. Every time he stood up to look above the water, he saw the same corridor he had been swimming through.

Maanvir: {slamming his hand in water} UGH what should I do? The temperature of the water is also dropping.

Magic He then noticed small waves forming as he used his voice.

Maanvir: ADHIRAJJJJ?

Suddenly, a wave formed and surged in the opposite direction. He shook his head and continued swimming until the wave disappeared. Then, he stopped and shouted his name, and the same thing happened again. After the repetition of the same incident, he finally reached a huge pool of water. He saw a Man sitting and praying in the end of pool

Maanvir: ADHIRAJJ??? IS THAT YOU?

Adhiraj: YES! OMG MAANVIR YOURE HERE.

Suddenly, all the water vanished as if it had turned into vapor and dried up. Both of them found themselves standing in an empty room with a glass wall behind them.

Adhiraj: {turning around} Hey is that, Alishka? And wait that's Himanshu?

Over here Alishka had already completed her maze and was in the middle where Himanshu was lying on the ground, his hands entangled in the roots of trees. Surrounding him, three team of crabs formed a circle with one meter gap between them, poised to devour him at any moment.

Alishka: {panicking} Oh my god, what am I supposed to do?

Himanshu: {shouting}ALISHKA! YOU NEED TO GRAB THAT KNIFE, OR ELSE THESE CRAB MIGHT FINISH ME, MAKE IT FAST PLEASE.

Alishka: what? How am I supposed to get those? Ok ok calm down. I need 2 minutes.

Saying that she observed the surroundings, that was covered with trees and a small light shining. Suddenly she saw a long branch hanging in the middle.

She turned around and picked a tree trunk lying down.

Alishka: Himanshu, if I step on your face, I am sorry

Himanshu: {shocked} What?

Alishka took a deep breath and stepped carefully in the small spaces between each crap. Basically, she was walking on her toes. She took another step and successfully cleared the first circle. And with a lot of attention and Grave expression she cleared the second circle too. As she stepped into the third circle, her luck seemed to falter. Startled by a sudden loud noise from him, she lost her footing, slipping and inadvertently crushing one of the Crab beneath her boot, turning the third circle into a scene of chaos. As the crabs sensed her presence, they swarmed, launching a relentless attack, stinging her legs and hands. Initially shielded by her thick leather jacket, she didn't register the pain. However, soon enough, agony pierced through as the stings penetrated her footwear, causing unbearable pain in her feet. In agony, she cried out and fought back, desperately attempting to punch or fling away every crab that encroached upon her, determined to shield her face from their relentless assault. Although she managed to protect her face and hands, her legs were in terrible condition. She cried out in pain, desperately calling for help. She frantically searched for something to defend herself with and fortunately stumbled upon the same stick she had picked up earlier. With a surge of determination, she gripped the branch tightly and, using its leverage, swung herself into the air, causing the crabs to scatter and freeing herself from their relentless assault.

As she grasped the knife tightly, it began to shimmer with an otherworldly light. In a surreal turn of events, all the crabs suddenly descended and vanished into thin air, as if fleeing from the radiant glow emanating from the blade.

Himanshu: {relieved} Thank God, you didn't step on my face.

Alishka: Thank God, they didn't sting you.

Without hesitation, she swiftly cut through the roots binding him, setting him free. As the last root was severed, a mystical energy surged, causing all the trees to dissolve into the air, leaving behind a sense of liberation and awe. After Himanshu was also transferred to the same room where Adhiraj and Maanvir were present, they hugged each other and a sense of relief casted over the face. But it swung away, after seeing Alishka still present there. Everyone was unsure of it, but then they remembered that Ahaan is still there, and Alishka need to save him.

Himanshu: I feel like this trip has made fall into a deep ditch and talking of Alishka! She already going through a lot and this?

Saying this he softly slammed his head in the glass and feeling guilty.

Adhiraj: {keeping his hand on his shoulder} Look we know it's our fault but trust me if we save this village people. We will accomplish one more thing in life.

Himanshu: If it was our dream or our thing, then we should be suffering not her, from the start of our friendship we have always protected her and.......

Alishka{interrupting}: Himanshu? No need to feel guilty. In fact, because of you guys I was able to save my sister Aleena. And if you guys have always saved me. It's my job now to get you all safe out of here. And yes, we all are team, don't you remember? What are we? Everybody with me.

Everyone: SHADOW HUNTERS

Alishka: {tears in her eyes} Yes, we are! Thank you for bringing it back. And now it's time to save someone I love deeply.

Adhiraj: {smirking} Yes, you do!

Alishka: {shouting} DRAVILLAAAAAAA! Am ready!

CHALLENGE 3: Love Gas

As she spoke those word, she heard two claps, and all the lights went out leaving in deadly darkness.

Distorted sound: You have five minutes to find your partner or else this gas might finish you and him he is here and there in the same corridor, Find him. Your time starts now.

Suddenly a gas started filling in the air. Listening to its sound she started running opposite to the direction.

Alishka: {panicking} AHAAAAN! Where are you? Ahaan!

As Ahaan heard her voice, he got up and the noise of gas in the air didn't go unnoticed by him.

Ahaan: Alishkaaaaaa! Am here! Alishkaaaaaa.

Suddenly something kicked his mind. He closed his eye and remembered Aliksha face and then...

"Alishka?"

Alishka: Huh who's that?

'Alishka, it's me Ahaan'

Alishka: Oh god Ahaan! I missed your voice so much where are you? Please I can't stay away from you anymore.

Ahaan: {contacting Alishka through his mind} Hey just listen to me, calm down. I need you to listen to me, this is a really big alley ok. I am at the end of the alley, and I need to come over there as there is something holding me back.

Alishka: Ok underst....

She began coughing and choking violently as the gas enveloped her, blocking her nostrils and leaving her gasping for each breath. Panic-stricken, she sprinted aimlessly into the darkness, desperate to escape the suffocating fumes. With every step, her vision blurred further, yet she pressed on, driven by the primal instinct to survive.

Here, his patience wore thin as he listened to her coughing, but an unnatural force gripped him, rendering him immobile. Despite his efforts to remain calm, the relentless pull of this mysterious force exacerbated his growing frustration. Her vulnerable state stirred a primal aggression within him, struggling against the invisible shackles constraining his every move. She sprinted blindly into the darkness, desperately fleeing the gas.

Unfortunately, she collided headfirst with an unseen obstacle, sending her sprawling onto her back. Pain shot through her as her head throbbed from the impact. Wincing in agony, she gritted her teeth, the pain from her already injured legs now compounded by the throbbing ache in her head. Every movement sent waves of discomfort through her body, but she knew she had to press on, despite the obstacles and the pain.

Hearing her cries of pain, he couldn't bear it any longer. A tear escaped his eyes as he felt a surge of restlessness and helplessness. Despite his own struggle against the mysterious force holding him back, he managed to find his voice, urging her to stay strong amidst the darkness and uncertainty.

Unable to stand, she resorted to crawling through the oppressive darkness, each jagged rock on the ground sending a jolt of pain through her already battered legs. Tears streamed down her cheeks; her vulnerability laid bare in the face of the relentless obstacles before her. Yet, amidst her suffering, her thoughts remained steadfast on him, consumed by the singular determination to find a way to save him.

Once more, she stumbled, her face colliding with the unyielding ground, her lips splitting and blood trickling down her chin. Trapped in her agony, she remained immobilized, tears mingling with the blood as she cried out in pain and frustration. With sheer willpower, she managed to drag herself a few inches farther, but the weight of her injuries and the despair of her situation bore down on her.

Closing her eyes, she allowed herself to be consumed by memories of him, each recollection a bittersweet reminder of what she was fighting for. Yet, in her darkest moment, she couldn't shake the overwhelming sense of defeat, feeling as though she had reached the limits of her strength and ability to save him.

Alishka: {crying} Ahaan I am sorry! I couldn't save you; I am sorry.

Ahaan: Aliksha? Alishka?

Alishka: no, no I can't, am sorry.

Ahaan: [holding her hands} Alishu alishu, just listen to me.

Feeling his touch, she stirred, her eyes fluttering open to behold a dark figure standing nearby. In an instant, light flooded the space, dispelling the suffocating gas, and there he stood before her, his charming smile illuminating the darkness. Relief washed over her as she gazed at him, a glimmer of hope reigniting within her weary heart.

Alishka: Oh my god! It's you. Come here. I missed Ahaan.

In a heartbeat, she enveloped him in a tight embrace, tears streaming down her cheeks as she buried her face in his shoulder. He returned the embrace, holding her close, his hand gently cradling her head. A profound sense of relief washed over both of them, the weight of their ordeal lifting in the presence of each other, as if seeing each other again after an eternity apart. Feeling his embrace tighten, she sensed his reluctance to let go, and in response, she nestled deeper into the warmth of his chest, finding solace in his protective hold. In that moment, it was as if the outside world ceased to exist, their bond reaffirmed by the simple act of holding each other close, finding strength in their shared embrace.

Ahaan: just never leave my hand ever again. I can't afford to lose you.

As they reluctantly released from their embrace, they gazed at each other, tears mingling with warm smiles.

However, his smile faded as his eyes took in the bruises and cuts marring her face and legs. Though the wounds were hers, he felt the pain as if it were his own, a deep ache resonating within him at the sight of her suffering. Without a word, he swiftly swept her into his arms, holding her close as he carried her out of the darkness and into the safety of the open air. In his embrace, she found comfort and security, knowing that together they would face whatever challenges lay ahead.

Epilogue

The glass wall disappeared and Adhiraj and Himanshu were also finally free. They ran behind the two and got out of darkness.

Adhiraj: {mischievously} Ahem! Ahaan? Where's Alishka.

Listening to his voice he swiftly made Alishka stand on her feet's and giving her support by holding her hand.

Himanshu: Oh, there she is.

Maanvir: Hey, Alisha are you okay, seeing those crab attacking you made me scared. Oh my god your legs are already bleeding, and wait is that a bruise in the side of your lips.

Alishka: Yeah, I just got bumped while running.

Ahaan: wait those bruises are given by crabs? But why are they bleeding?

Alishka: I don't know maybe they didn't only sting but tried to rip off my skin.

Adhiraj: But guys where are we?

Listening to that everyone finally observed the surroundings and found themselves standing at the middle of the two caves with only trees and blue evening sky above.

Himanshu: Look over there, the third entrance about which Daaniya told us.

Alishka: The only entrance which connects the two caves.

Over here Saina and Aleena were exploring the forest when they heard small commotion and talking. they followed the voice and it led to same entrance.

Maanvir: Saina? Omg is that you?

As everyone looked outside and spotted them standing there, a wave of relief washed over the onlookers. He rushed towards her, enveloping her in a tight hug, their embrace a symbol of their survival and resilience. Tears of joy filled the eyes of those gathered, grateful to see each and every member alive and safe after the harrowing ordeal.

Adhiraj and Himanshu rushed towards Saina. But Aliksha was having a little difficulty in walking. Ahaan gently supported her, holding her shoulders as she took short, steady steps.

Saina: OMG Alishka? What happened to you?

She ran towards her, pushing Ahaan aside and hugged her tightly.

Saina: {breaking the hug} Am so sorry babe, that I didn't ask how you are and straight away ordered you to save Maanvir. I feel like a bad friend

Alishka: {cupping her face} Its ok Saina, I understand. Even I was in you state {adverting her gaze towards Ahaan} I would have taken his name, because even at the time of the danger we remember the person we care for the most and don't want to lose.

Listening to her, Ahaan just gave a small smile, and adverted his attention towards the boys. They all walked a little far from the cave and now were standing at the edge of the land which was again Facing the waterfall.

Alishka: {smiling} BTW are you ok? I mean what actually happened when you were inside? Did you get any dream or any vision?

Saina: Talking of vision, you forgot about you sister, I guess.

Alishka: {realizing} I am so sorry. OMG Aleena.

Saying that she ran towards Aleena who was standing in the corner, quietly observing everyone with a small smile forming in her lips but her mind and heart ingulfed with guilty all over. Alishka enveloped Aleena in a tight heartfelt embrace. To which Aleena didn't reciprocate just stood there speechless and drowned in guilty and shock.

Alishka: {breaking the hug} OMG Aleena look at you, she has so miserably tortured my sister. OMG, I thought I lost you forever. But all my prayer and Pujas are answered. Mom will be finally happy to see you after....

Aleena: {tears dwelling} Please......Don't say that...you know what the reality.

Ahaan: {interrupting} No Aleena, that where you're wrong. All your life you had a thought that your parents hated you. But you know what actually happened when you left?

Alishka: Ahaan that's enough, she is not in the stage to know everything. Just stop the topic over here.

Ahaan simply shrugged his Sholder and left the sister alone. Alishka just scanned all over her body and seeing are the bruises and marks marrying her skin, boiled her blood more than anything. Aleena just stared at the ground as the guilt weighted heavy on Sholder. Suddenly she felt a slight grasp on her Sholder and Glanced over Alishka, who standing over there and glaring at her with a single tear streaming down her eye.

Alishka: WHY? I JUST WANNA ASK WHY? WHY DID YOU DO IT?

Hearing her shout everyone shifted their attention towards her and were taken aback by that sight. Aleena was too stunned to speak; all she could do was stare at the ground with guilt hugely hanging on her Sholder.

Alishka: {shaking her} Just tell me why did make me suffer? No, the real question is, WHY DID YOU MAKE

YOURSELF SUFFER? HUH? No Aleena I want an answer, just because of our parents you started hating on me and refusing the fact, that I have always been kind to you. You started hating me so much that you wanted me dead?

Aleena: {whimpering} Look, I was wrong......please.... i never understood. Your love for me....

Alishka: {smiling sarcastically} So...... ITS true! You did go in the cave, just to end me and win love of our parents you never or you think you never received!

Saina: {interrupting} Alishka, it's not the time.... you've only told Ahaan to stop earlier.

Aleena: {crying} I am sorry, hatred, jealousy and anger made me ....

Alishka: Hatred, jealously, anger! That too with your own sister, who always tried her best...... you know what, if that what's you wanted, that would've given you peace, then fine. I will give you peace.

Saying that, she started walking towards the end, startling everyone who began shouting her name. Before she could get very far, she felt a firm, urgent grasp on her elbow, halting her steps. She turned to find him holding her tightly, his eyes filled with a mix of concern. As their eyes locked, he pulled her closer with determination, their faces inches apart, the air between them charged with unspoken emotions. Everyone was relieved to see her safe, but as he pulled her closer, they all discreetly turned away and walked further, giving them the privacy they needed.

Ahaan: {aggressively whispering}: DON'T YOU DARE! DON'T YOU DARE TAKE ANY WRONG STEP LIKE THESE!

Alishka: Am sorry, I just got carried away.

After that, they were both lost in each other's eyes, unable to confess the feelings locked in their hearts. The world around them faded away, leaving only the unspoken emotions that bound them together.

Over there, they were all engrossed in chatting and discussing their next steps to escape. She sat quietly in the corner, tears streaming down her face, consumed by guilt. As she watched them immersed in their conversations, she felt like a burden, an outsider in their world. Quietly, she attempted to sneak away, hoping to escape the weight of her remorse alone.

Unbeknownst to her, as she tried to sneak away, an unknown force full of light and wind came flying towards her. It stopped her in her tracks, its brilliance and power captivating everyone present. She stood there, stunned and unable to move, as the force enveloped her, drawing the attention and awe of everyone around. That supernatural force transformed into a woman wearing a colorful saree. As she opened her eyes, they shone brightly, causing everyone to shield their eyes from the intense light. The woman's presence was both awe-inspiring and otherworldly, commanding the attention and reverence of all who were there.

Daaniya: It's me, guys you all can open your eyes now.

Adhiraj: Daaniya? What are you doing here? And would you care to explain all the chaos?

Himanshu: Maa ji was the one behind all this and we didn't have any idea?

Saina: {shocked} Wait Maa ji is behind all this?

Daaniya: Ok ok! Calm down, Look I never knew that Maa ji was behind it but am neither shocked. I hope you all are safe, because we need your help! And where's Alishka?

Over here Ahaan and Aliksha were sitting at the edge of the land with their feet's hanging in the air. Ahaan was gazing at the waterfall while Aliksha being lost in her own world.

Ahaan: You've changed a lot.

Alishka just looked at him with uncertainty and shrugged her Sholders.

Ahaan: I mean, what happened that made you the older version of me?

Alishka: {smirking} What made you be that way?

Ahaan: {scoffs} Where's that girl who said that she will never change no matter how life is cruel towards her?

Alishka: I can ask the same question to you too.

Maanvir: {shouting} Ahaan and Alisha, you need to see this.

Both of them just took a deep breath and got up from there. Followed Maanvir where other people descended.

Daaniya: Oh, there you are Alishka. I am really proud of you. And I think its time you all should leave Alanchal and save your lives.

Alishka: NO! We can't! We need to save Alanchal.

Ahaan: What do you mean? Daaniya: LOOK! Alishka, its better if you all leave and save your lives.

Saina: {interrupting} And if we are gone, who's going to save Alanchal and these innocent people?

Daaniya: You can't save, or I should say you can defeat dravilla because Maa ji is with her the ashram is in her hands and you don't even have your device or strength or knowledge.

Alishka: {smirking} That's where you're wrong. Because I have something that you don't have Daaniya and not even any of you have.

Adhiraj: But before that we need to get out of here as its going to rain and we need shelter.

Alishka: There is a small hut nearby, we can take shelter over there.

Everyone just looked at her with uncertainty.

Saina: Yes, there is nearby, I saw it when Dravilla held me up in air.

Alishka: Follow me

As they walked on, everyone trailed behind her, a sense of uncertainty and confusion lingering in the air. After covering a solid kilometer, they stumbled upon a quaint hut, eliciting shocked expressions from everyone present.

Alishka: Let's enter.

Everyone obediently followed her instructions and entered the hut.